To Ma

I hope you will
enjoy this book...

Ellison & Amos
(Inspired by a true story)

Charlie Gibbons

Charlie Gibbons

" Some are born
to move the World. "

Without which we'd
be eternally stuck...

DEDICATED

to my beloved son. You are my past, present, and future.

CONTENTS

"There's no replacing any member of **this** band."
- Geddy Lee

ACKNOWLEDGEMENTS

I would like to acknowledge the inspired works of Jack London, and The Sea Wolf specifically, which excerpts appear in this work, published by Dover Publications.

Likewise, the compiled works and experience of other writers who become a part of who we are, and shape who we become by their inspired words...

Something that's not worth losing
Is nothing you've missed so easy
Time is a bitter friend
And pain its strongest tool

I wish I could blot out the memories
By means objective and stereotyped
But what's the point of proving to myself
That you're not worth the fight

I constantly repeat these habits
Of trying to get it right
If love wasn't at the end of the rainbow
Then there wouldn't be a goal in sight

Nothing is what I have without you
And something I can't give up
Change is my best friend
Without which I'd be eternally stuck

Inside every mind is the content of a different Hollywood Studio. We all don't see the same movie....

If love is the only thing that can change us, then if we're incapable of love, we're incapable of change. Without love we are dead inside.

Chapter One

1975

There wasn't anything distinguishable about him. He was just like any other boy. He was average height. He was neither more handsome for an eleven year old, or scrawny in disposition compared to other 5th graders. He loved kickball, and recess, and on occasion even had a crush on a little girl his age. But to the other children, something was already beginning to define him, make him stand out. It was only his homeroom class who saw it.

"What did I say to the teacher this morning?" he thought in line for tether ball.

There was no right or wrong in his mind. It was literal. A boy's predisposition at this age wasn't developed in the school of self-reflection beyond the innocent realms of the day to day. Take out the trash, and pick up your room were the only requirements. An occasional "don't pick on your sister" when she ventured into his territory. The parental repercussions were never severe for any infraction, but cut and dry.

Having studied the explorers for the past month, his teacher asked which of them they liked most. When Ellison raised his hand, she called on him because of the force of the thrust his arm leapt into the air.

"I'd have to say Hernando Cortez," he responded smartly, as a matter of fact.

"And why is that, Ellison?"

Her question was like a tennis ball, rebounding back at him, and he replied almost mechanically.

"His insouciance about conquering the Aztecs."

For just a millisecond the teacher's eyes lit up, then subsided.

"What he means class is, Cortez was so sure of himself, that he didn't doubt his success. Insouciance means a lack of concern, so he wasn't concerned at all about victory. Does anyone know why?"

The teacher went on, and Ellison put his head down as a kid next to him giggled, then looked at another classmate to utter a word they all knew.

"Freak."

Ellison lost the tether ball game and another took his place as he left the circle. Then an impression so strong hit him in the back of the head that time stopped, as it always does when something traumatic happens. His hand instinctively moved there, and he turned to see a classmate named Bobby laugh as he retrieved the baseball that ricocheted off his head. Ellison stood bewildered as the boy, smaller than he, ran away.

Why?

Tears welled up in his eyes, not because of pain, for there was none, but because of the act. Two little girls shouted "Ellison's hurt" to the teacher on duty, and he felt the quiver of his lip, his body uncontrollably sent a signal to his brain that it was real.

Whisking conglomerations of bright colors contagious to the styles of clothes at the time congregated around him. Then he was brushed away, guided by the gentle arm around his shoulder, as the throng of onlookers reached its peak, and like the stroke of a brush handle across the canvas, the procession flowed his direction out of the yard.

But he never told who had done the terrible deed.

Chapter Two
1988

She worked as fast as she could. There was an edginess inside she couldn't explain or put her finger on. The 31 year old woman was serious in her task, and it was total devotion and love that drove her. She placed the plastic bag sealed with a twist-tie into the cart. Rounding the corner she moved to the next aisle. The list played over and over in her mind like the rehashed events of a day, playing like a broken record against a scratch.

The woman looked back toward the windows at the front of the grocery store. The sun and distance to the parking lot made it impossible to discern detail, but she glanced out over again nonetheless. She was suddenly distracted, smiled wide and longingly at an item. She picked up the bib with a picture of a lion nuzzling his cub, and her thoughts were again on the task at hand. She placed it in the cart carefully, on top of other items. Who knew what germs lurked on the metal containing her prizes.

The woman entered the frozen food section with her back to the sun as another woman rushed into the store and up to management in a frenzy. Shrimp, green beans, pie shells, and a pizza supreme were added to the cart. She strategically placed them together against the canned food. Next, she found her husband's favorite steak, Foster Farm chicken, and her one luxury, a quart of eggnog. She felt a warm glow wash through her with the approaching holidays. Secretly she admired the market for carrying the item so early in October.

Another 5 minutes passed, and she was on the juice aisle when a man touched her shoulder from behind.

"Are you Beverly?"

Before a word left her lips, the Assistant Manager read the look of confirmation in her body language.

"You better follow me."

Suddenly the piercing noise of a siren reverberated through the glass of the windows, and the woman broke ahead of the man frantically. Outside, she immediately covered the distance to where her son and husband were awaiting her return. A crowd of people huddled around one side of the car. She broke through with a mad look in her eyes, and an adoring expression on her mouth, accentuated by her lovely, petite form.

"Amos!" she cried.

Her 2 year old boy lay crying on the ground, his fragile little head supported by her husband. The shriek of his voice was more than she could bear, replacing the man's support with her own.

The voice from above her stated he'd fallen out of the car, but she didn't register the close relationship to its owner.

"Mommy! Mommy!" was uttered from her palms, cutting through the sensory overload of this scene. She didn't notice the paramedics who rushed their equipment inside the circle of onlookers.

Her eyes finally met the man responsible for watching out for her boy as she stood above the men now caring for him. In those eyes she saw something she'd never seen before. It was something so terrible to her world that their relationship would change forever through all the years ahead. It was ambivalence. Just a millisecond passed and then left as he became aware he'd given something away. Tears welled up in her, tears of disappointment, betrayal, and instinct.

"One of his arms is broken, ma'am. And one leg. The hospital will be able to tell us more. He must have fallen feet over head, the force of impact moved up his body."

Several hours later, her husband stood quietly against the wall of the hallway in the ER, his forehead in contact with the panels.

"Look at me," she said startling him.

He stood up, small in comparison despite his foot height over hers.

She looked at him for a long half minute before continuing. Her expression softened, and the anger left her. His lips parted, as if about to speak. But he knew she'd seen his secret.

"I love you. Maybe more than you love yourself. But this is our one chance to have a future. Do you hear me?"

He just nodded.

"If anything ever, ever happens to my little boy again, I will leave you and take your unborn daughter, and never see you again. Do you understand me?"

"Yes," he said unsure how to regulate the volume in his voice.

She stared at him a moment, and then nodded her head.

"Come inside when you're able."

She slowly turned and entered the room across from where they stood. The light went out of his eyes again, like in the parking lot. He stood looking where she'd disappeared expressionless.

No matter what was said that day, Beverly never left her precious boy alone with his father, except on rare instances. When Amos' sister was born, she arranged for family from out of town for help. The bond between him and his mother became more prevalent. Had it not been for that day, who knew what the differences would be?

Chapter Three
Masculinity

It was evening before they gathered around the card table. The whiskey and poker was to pacify Rowdy so that the next two days could be devoted to hiking and camping. The setting was perfect. A long room with an unused stone fireplace at one end, pictures of westerns with Hollywood stars long gone occupying each space of wall, touches of rustic wood furniture and rocking chairs, and broad bookcases wrapped around a fair sized television in the middle next to the card table. Other patrons at the Dow Villa, a motel with an air of modesty and history, laughed and admired the vivacity of the ongoing card games and the ravenous cursing each time Rowdy lost as the evening progressed.

Like musketeers of old, the four had pledged not to let a year go by before each annual reprise, and that leaving college wouldn't allow the world to take over their youth. The week of adventure had been postponed a month because of Shane's marital problems, and Rowdy's European binge. The time would be made up easily, but not without the typical drama, especially where Rowdy was concerned.

The four friends had settled on Las Vegas as their playground, then changed locales to Mount Whitney, which is on the northwest side of Death Valley in California. Ted had concocted the plan so he and Dave could manipulate Rowdy from an airplane to Los Angeles to a car ride to Lone Pine, CA without any objections 'til the 3 hour drive was complete.

"You sons of bitches," Rowdy stated out of the blue as they began their 8th hand.

"Wonder who he could be speaking to, Dave," stated Ted without looking up from his cards, and without a smirk where one could easily be imagined.

"Fucker," said Rowdy without a second to lose, peering at his cards like a super hero focusing his death rays on an arch enemy.

"You start, Rowdy," stated Shane flatly.

"I know you didn't know anything about this. Did you?" the blame finally making its way from Ted, to Dave, and finally to Shane.

A slight restraint registered in his voice toward Shane that didn't in the others. Despite Rowdy's tough exterior, they were real friends. Not the superficial bullshit heard from campus halls, or emails between colleagues that want something from each other, afraid to burn a bridge because it might develop into a business contact 5 or 10 years down the road.

There was a price Shane had paid for Rowdy's loyalty; genuine compassion. Shane and Rowdy were roommates in college, and had it not been for the selfless nagging that Rowdy complete papers, and prepare for tests, he would not have passed. Rowdy was far from stupid, just obviously hard to motivate.

Rowdy knew that Shane didn't expect anything in return, and would never speak of it, any more than he would the time Rowdy set a pile of toilet paper on fire on the lawn in high school.

"It was Shane's idea," replied Dave smiling ear to ear.

"Bullshit," responded Rowdy.

Dave broke into a full blown laugh, as if the cat hadn't already been let out of the bag.

"Come on. Let's just make the best of it and have a good time," said Ted.

They were all waiting for Rowdy to decide whether he needed a card, or to place a bet.

"Do you think a card game can make up for the women we're missing in Vegas?"

Ted was the practical anchor in the foursome, neither austere, nor prudish in manner, but somewhat 'Spockish.'

"What difference does it make to us, Rowdy?" he replied.

"Well, you can still appreciate a gorgeous woman, can't you?

"I'm going to admit something to you, Rowdy," said Dave. "I hate fake boobs. Not to mention tattoos. What the hell has happened to the world? You don't put a bumper sticker on a friggin' Mercedes, or Lexus."

"What are you talking about?" replied Rowdy.

"He's talking about taste, Rowdy," said Ted. "We like what we've always liked. We haven't changed. Why do you think our wives have gym memberships?"

This brought a snigger out of Shane. Despite all the problems with his wife, she cared about keeping herself in shape, and at one time he thought she was the prettiest of the three wives.

"So it's finally come to this, huh? You three are going to force me out because I'm not married to some trophy wife. Well, fuck that. I'm not going to end up like my parents and find myself in separate beds in thirty years. No way in hell."

"Rowdy. Settle down," said Ted. "We love you, man. No one's trying to force you out. Why do you think we told you we were going to Vegas?"

"So I'll get pissed off and refuse to come along," he shouted.

Shane stepped in. His voice was strong, and even. He and Ted were a lot alike, but he let Ted be the mouthpiece for the group. It was just his way, like in college.

"Rowdy. Do you know what makes someone special?"

Rowdy's facial muscles froze, and he put his cards face down on the table. Had they been face up, the other three would now have had something to be concerned about.

"Being special without being told you are. Knowing it, feeling it. A woman is special because she just is. You can love her, but you can't teach her to be something she isn't. It's like America. She started off with the right idea, but she was corrupted by slavery, and eventually became self-absorbed like England was."

Dave slipped a comment under his breath.

"King Shane has entered the building," smiling.

"You have to find balance," Shane resumed," or you're just a bad circus act. I hope we're there when you find it."

There was a pause. Ted leaned forward and broke the seal on a new whiskey bottle, and poured them all a shot. Rowdy was the first to down his, and slam the glass on the table. He picked up the cards, and slid two to Shane, who had dealt. Shane took two off the top, and put them next to Rowdy's hand.

Ted, then Dave played, but Shane dropped the first chip into the center of the table. His glass of whiskey remained full for some time...

8

Chapter Four
Time & Motion

The familiar mountains surrounded his home like a reminder of every fond memory of the past 15 glorious years. Once what was the beauty of the Rocky Mountains of Colorado were now like the piercing, stabbing motion of ice shards as they fell into vulnerable flesh, raw from months of cold, wear and tear spanning four winters with no spring, summer, or autumn. The mind knows nothing about the loss he experienced, because it played tricks on him continually. It played on the routine of life, expecting habits no longer possible. The shock made more poignant each time he imagined hearing the voices, as if the very thought of them could recreate what was no more, by shear will.

His heart on the other hand, knew all too well the reality that made each day like a love song that played on and on, and never reaching climax of chorus or changing tempo. His heart would continually remind the mind there was no place his body could go to find them. No plane could fly to them, and no drive in vehicles which shared many of the memories that echoed the hollow halls and chambers of his broken heart.

Hope had departed across that mythological river. He had to leave, or the insanity would stop his blood from pumping, lungs from breathing anything but the poison of his depressed thoughts. His ears still heard the cries of happiness at every turn. He had to replace them. He couldn't be where he saw first steps, songs around the tree, or kisses of loving affection.

Ellison's gear was packed on the motorcycle with the essentials for the trip, his home finally behind him.

Should I look back?

He knew the road ahead, and wanted more than anything to cover as much of that familiar ground as possible. He began rounding the bend of the lone dirt road of his property, but kept his eyes front.

All I need is distance and motion.

With this small success, he almost broke down right there, but this would cause him to have to pull over and remove his helmet. That would delay things. It would take another hour just to get to the freeway from the obscure parcel of land that had totally lost value to him now.

"No!" he shouted, his voice vibrating and amplifying around his head.

He reached the I-70, and headed west. It was late, 1 pm. The hum of the wheels on the road was soothing, and consistent with the numbness now in his head. He couldn't go fast enough, and wished he could push the cycles speed to 100, but that would be noticeable, so he kept it at 75. The Eisenhower tunnel, Glenwood Springs, and finally Grand Junction, Colorado passed. He barely noticed them. Utah had never been such a pleasant sight. He drove 'til it was 10:30 pm.

He came across a little town, no idea its name. He knew his stomach was empty, but the impulse to sleep was greater. There would always be breakfast. He showered unceremoniously, the light from the room showing the way in the dark of the motel bath. The only gratification was washing the sweat of the day off. He awoke at 5:45 am, dressed and brushed his teeth. There was a Burger King open, and he remembered their sausage croissants being particularly good from some time back. He ate and drank his coffee while straddling the bike, surprised at how much satisfaction it gave him. It made him forget the billows upon waking, muffled into the pillow just minutes ago.

Approaching the I-15 was almost more than he could take. Had he gone south, his heart might have exploded in his chest. How many shows had they played from Vegas to L.A.? Ellison's perception of them changed largely since the names of these venues changed reflecting the companies who later bought them, rather than the community that inspired their construction. His desire to drive north was as intense as his need to leave the place he'd spent the most significant part of his life. But the farther he got the tighter his chest got, as if he were betraying the people he'd loved and lost. Leaving the place his memories lingered was his salvation and pain.

What a paradox.

It was August, and perfect weather to drive to Alaska; then who knows where. He was being chased by a ghost, and knew he just had to make it past Salt Lake City. The weather was hot, and the sweat inside his clothes was the only part of him that did not reflect the numbness now. Lost was his passion for trees, birds, and animals. The constant 'hum' of the engine was the music of Ellison's future, more so than concerts and studios.

The road continually replaced these thoughts. He suddenly laughed out loud on some portion of highway along the Oregon Trail in Idaho passing a gorgeous section of the Snake River. The day was going by, a blur.

Where did that come from? I am losing my mind?

He continued to smile.

Am I like the dumb animal spoken of by Thoreau, blinders keeping my attention forward, neither looking from this side to that?

The over-thought of philosophy was as ridiculous as any attention to the details he left behind as the terrain changed. But he could not deny that it was still a part of his identity.

How comforting to be that mule leading a wagon? More than the teamster, 'wending his way to market.' All around me, the world carries on. Economics, political feuding, competition, anger and hate. I don't care. Rather be, just be...

His existence was no one's business but his own. More than ever, his individuality was central to the future. No one was responsible for his salvation, mental or physical.

The thought of typical contrivances with clergy and modes of therapy were inconceivable. His eyes caught hold of the lines in the road again, and Ellison became lost, caught in a meditative trance. The break in the lines, a breathe, or heart beats. Light years in time, as it were, the speed of thought having no relevance to the echoes of those still in his life, those all around caring about past, present, and future. Who knew how long before he returned, and what condition the world would be in at that future date?

He admitted to himself that the path which was once the Oregon Trail was impressive, almost ideal and picturesque, if not for being under the watchful eye of the freeway. He didn't stop until Washington. It was around 9:00 pm when the motorcycle pulled up to a Denny's in Lacey, great anticipation in a meal, and the peace away from the lines which finally became monotonous. Sitting at a booth near the back corner of the restaurant, menu in hand, it dawned on him that his last meal was early that morning. This was comforting for some reason. It wasn't the first time in the past five months he'd neglected to eat.

11

Normal, considering?

The next day flashed in his head, and he had a productive thought.

The Sea Wolf.

It was in his gear on the cycle.

I will start it tomorrow.

The anticipation was as tangible as dinner. He ordered the turkey and mashed potatoes. He couldn't explain why it looked so good.

Another day gone.

It was over. He had nothing to do but check into a motel, and crash for the night. The waitress brought him a cold, fresh beer in a glass. He sipped it luxuriously, another first in five months. The alcohol wasn't important. It was a sign that Ellison's mourning was progressing.

He looked out the window at the lights and traffic. He knew the lush green landscape was waiting for him come morning. The forecast was clear throughout the week, a short summer expected by all who waited patiently, and knowing that it was the price to pay for such beauty.

He was in no hurry to reach British Columbia, Canada. No large feat at all from Lacey. The peninsula was his goal, and a place he never had time to visit. He'd played in Seattle many times. It was no comparison to the Olympic rain forest, littered with quaint towns to stop for a tank of gas, and lose himself in the novel he'd been looking forward to by Jack London.

The beer was half gone when his food arrived. The taste of the mashed potatoes and gravy were like the first time he'd tasted lobster, and every time since. It then reminded him of last Thanksgiving which had been routine, more for the want of family and friends.

A faint smile appeared on his face, and then at its peak, faded fast, and a tear welled up in one eye, running its course down his cheek. Ellison wiped it away as if swatting away a fly. Four college students entered the restaurant, uttering the latter half of some conversation that began outside.

"... but he didn't know we were standing there. Suddenly, Troy turned and saw us stuck together like two pieces of a puzzle, and punches Ed in the shoulder," continued a student wearing a Pittsburgh

12

Steelers t-shirt. "I swear, I look over as he turns around, and sees us. The whole room goes quiet."

They took a booth parallel to Ellison's.

"I wish I'd had it on my camera phone, cuz dude, his eyes filled up like some bitch watching a soap opera."

They all laughed, eyes casing the place instinctively, wanting for the attention of a crowd not present.

"Sentimental bastard," said a kid across from the storyteller. "If I ever get like that, put me in an old folks home with all the rest of the diaper wearing old shits."

Ellison couldn't help hearing their conversation and tried to pretend he was still in his own world as he took a fork and knife to the slices of turkey.

"He was in my English class our freshman year. Girls swooned like crazy every time he read his damn poetry," said the biggest guy, leaning back against the wall nonchalantly.

"Liz wasn't making out with me because I read her poetry."

The Steelers fan lifted his right arm, and flexed. His friends nodded agreeably.

Ellison shook his head instinctively, and then caught himself. If there was ever a time to reveal his identity, like Clark Kent transforming into Superman, this would be it. He was uncharacteristically tempted as a writer of lyrics himself, so much so that he even saw the whole thing play out in vivid detail. How had his lyrics, paralleled with his guitar playing, made little school girls of even the most macho of men?

"Hey. Is that your bike outside?"

Ellison was suddenly pulled into the present.

"Yeah, you," stated the fellow relating the story.

Ellison looked back at his food and nodded in affirmation.

"I thought all you ol' farts rode Harley's."

Ol' fart?

He was surprised at the college student's blunt rudeness. Ellison was used to seeing himself this way, from the inside, but not others. He didn't look old. The band attracted all ages; rock musicians viewed having found the coveted fountain of youth. It reminded him of conversations with the band about the difference between fans who followed them because of their hard rock style and those who followed the lyrical themes. These brutes made him think of new fans that were drawn to the former.

"Let the man enjoy his food in peace boys," said the waitress who surprised everyone, including Ellison.

"Oh, hey. You scared us, mom," said the kid across from the football fan whose back was to the front of the restaurant.

"I'm not your mom. Are you here to eat?"

The waitress was young looking, 32 years old, but had a very mature aura. She was trim, and sleek with long brown hair pulled back in a pony tail, and lovely curves. Only the kid leaning against the wall noticed her beauty. Sometimes age had no bearing on a person physically, and this was particularly true with her.

Ellison hoped he would not have to defend her honor as he sipped at the beer, realizing the taste of the food had spoiled its richness.

"I didn't mean my mom. Heavens, she wouldn't find herself waiting tables while her kids are home baby-sitting themselves like yours," returned the smart mouthed kid.

The waitress stopped in her tracks, eyes narrowing. Ellison looked over at her, surveying the scene, and knew that what happened next would be decided by her reply.

"Okay, ladies," she finally said, pronouncing each syllable like a knife. "Either you apologize for your lack of manners, or I call the cops and have your asses hauled off. What would your weak little mommies say if they have to pick you up in the morning?"

"Let's fly," said the Steelers fan.

His friends followed quietly to their feet, and started for the front of the restaurant. The big one who leaned against the wall the entire time went over to Ellison's table and looked at his plate. Both froze a moment.

"The food's left over from last November anyway, Rory." He walked to his friends and they laughed, looking back at the waitress as they exited.

The waitress disappeared for at least 10 minutes, while Ellison recomposed his emotions, and finished his plate. She appeared quietly, approaching his table with purpose, and set a lovely piece of pumpkin pie with whip cream on it on the table.

He looked up into her smiling face.

14

"Sorry about the lousy entertainment. My boyfriend's a County Sheriff, and I just gave him their license number. He's very protective."

"I wish they hadn't said what they did. It was very snobbish."

"Oh, that. I don't have any kids. But if I did, and they ever acted like that, I'd take a coat hanger to 'em."

She smiled ear to ear.

"Enjoy your pie. It's on the house."

She turned and left.

The pie was excellent. They said "goodbye" at the register, a ten dollar bill next to the empty plates.

Chapter Five
The Old Man & the Sea

"Grab hold of something and hang on," the red-faced man said to me. All his bluster was gone, and he seemed to have caught the contagion of preternatural calm. "And listen to the women scream," he said grimly - almost bitterly, I thought, as though he had been through the experience before.
The vessels came together before I could follow his advice... The Martinez heeled over, sharply..." (The Sea Wolf page 6)

Ellison did not go to sleep immediately. He was too anxious, nervous, and lost in time. He also broke one of his lifelong rules by starting a book late at night, because he read until 1am when his eyes could not stay open any longer. Consequently, he woke at ten, rolled over and read a few more pages 'til reality set in, and then decided to shower and hit the road.

It took him two hours to drive north to Bremerton, the first place he wanted to visit. He actually got off the highway and went east out of the way. The alternative would have been through the cities lining Puget Sound into Seattle, and taking the ferry to Bremerton. The ferry ride was the only appealing aspect of that route.

The Olympic Peninsula was surrounded by Puget Sound on the east, the Straits of Juan de Fuca on the north separating the U.S. from Canada, and the Pacific Ocean on the west. The middle was all mountains and trees, cities and towns scattered the borders of the waterways. The geography of the land and mountains, hills and shoreline, were indescribable. No other part of western Washington was like the peninsula. Both exquisite, but different. Olympia and Tacoma was west & east points to the other on the southernmost part of the Sound. Ellison took the land route up the eastern side of the peninsula across the bridge.

He stopped at a Starbucks for a Chai Tea Latte, and walked to a beautiful perch overlooking the Sound as the Ferries came and went. The sun was warm, and the greenness from every plant big and small covered everything, including the cracks between the cement and rocks below the porch where he sat.

There were couples and friends sitting around, enjoying the late summer weather. Ellison basked in the laziness of the day, born by the late morning sleep, his feet up on the steel rail. He put his head back as the sun warmed his head of hair. Appropriately, he decided to wait until reaching the Yukon Territory before finishing his London book. His mind was searching to find something else to occupy it between here and there.

"Excuse me. Aren't you a musician?" came a voice from the next table.

Ellison awoke from his own thoughts, and looked over at the two younger men near him. His worst fear came alive. But he had to admit it was just a matter of time before being recognized.

"I used to be, but not anymore," he quickly responded.

"Yeah, but you were with..." The man addressing him stopped short to answer his cellular phone; the ring tone Zeppelin's "Stairway to Heaven."

"Saved by the bell," he thought, and without being obvious, put his baseball cap on, and slipped away down the steps which led to the Sound below.

The warm water around my world
Sing to me gently, rock me to sleep
I cannot see your face outside
My solitary bubble like an ocean deep

Transforming me to shapes and forms
A mind triggering wide ideas
Of colors remarkably green and blue
Awarding prizes far brighter than skies

Now I return - blood upon my head
And reasons my thoughts cannot believe
Your voice in memory the color of red
To where I clearly draw breath

17

We are born of water and blood from the womb
a metaphor in facets from life to death
It's no wonder we are connected
from Mesopotamia to the African mines

A consciousness privy to an awareness few
from enlightened to heretics in garden tombs

Ellison strolled along the shoreline, which was an impressive expanse in all directions, including the hill behind him. He noted mentally that it was more dramatic than an ocean because England or Japan was not visible to the east or west, and the horizon was an imaginative spot unclear to reality. But there, just a few miles away, was Seattle, and a gigantic glass parking lot with the potential of swallowing him up, contributing to his miniscule size. It was a stinging sensation to imagine death so dramatically.

The Sound disappeared both south and north, which made his finite nature like a mite and the frightening thought of being swallowed up surreal. These days the possibility of tsunamis seemed more real than ever.

Ellison had recurring nightmares in childhood of being sucked through something the size of a power outlet. His own screams awoke his parents, and his father had to uncharacteristically slap him into consciousness.

A ferry became visible, growing larger by the minute, and he retreated to a set of stairs which led to a cafe a hundred feet from where he descended.

It was 4:30 pm, and he was hungry for something simple. He entered the cafe and chose a sandwich and salad combo, with a bottle of cold water to clean the latte from his palette. Two men caught his attention upon exiting, sitting at a table next to the rail, playing chess. His curiosity was peaked.

He hadn't played since a teenager; taught by an uncle who visited his dad for 3 months at a time over the summer. How amazingly titillating to him now; getting lost in a three dimensional game of strategy and chance.

18

Ellison watched out of the corner of his eye from a table in the middle of the patio next to them, unaware of the process of eating, but only the act of finishing. He set his plate and bowl aside and turned their direction so he could observe their technique. That's all it really was to him. Any skill he had in his youth was demoted to the basic premise of how each piece moved.

A waitress appeared from the cafe and cleared away his dishes, absolving any reason to occupy the table. To his surprise, one of the two men turned and asked if he wanted to rotate in.

"Oh, thank you. I'd rather just watch. I haven't played in years."

"Pull your chair up, then," was the man's reply.

Ellison did so gladly. The men didn't introduce themselves, but it was clear they knew each other for quite some time. They didn't seem interested in Ellison, which made him more comfortable. Both of them were in their early thirties, tall, and in good physical shape.

"Shane snuck a letter into Rowdy's carryon bag when he wasn't looking, before he left," said the man in the red shirt. Ted slid it to Dave's side of the table,

"How'd you get it?"

"Rowdy faxed it the night they split up."

"Are we playing ball tomorrow?" said Dave making another move.

"Yeah. Holly is going to her sisters in Silverdale with the kids."

"Cool," was his reply. "Meet you at the ferry at 5:30?"

"K."

Ellison watched them play two games, noticing the mechanical way each began; the pawns that came out first, then the horse and bishop. Ted would direct certain moves to Ellison occasionally; instructionally. This included the "castle" maneuver, and subsequent "checks." He won both games.

"Checkmate."

Dave replied "good game" genuinely each time he lost. This surprised Ellison.

Was he expecting to lose, or did he really appreciate the competition between them?

"I'll be back in a few minutes," said Dave, snatching the letter from the table and entering the cafe.

19

"Come," Ted instructed.

Ellison moved to the seat across the table as the man returned the white pieces to their start position. He followed suit, putting the black pieces in their spots.

"Dave and I have been playing long enough, we forget the classic openings," he said. "So, I'll just give you a few rules I would keep in mind while playing."

"Cool," responded Ellison.

"My first rule is, be careful lining your king and queen up on the same line as the game unfolds. If you're checked, when you move the king, you can lose your queen as a trophy."

"Ahh."

"Number two. The person who can control 'check' after 'check,' will dominate the game, and his own strategy. You want to keep your opponent on the run. The more times you 'check' him, the less time he has to maneuver his own pieces."

"That's clever."

"Remember. It doesn't matter whether you win or lose. The more you play someone better than you, the better you'll get, accept my friend Dave. He's in a slump right now. Ready to play, then?" the man smiled.

Ellison paused briefly.

"Yeah," he stated emphatically.

Ted took his first turn, but it was not in the fashion Ellison witnessed before. The following game lasted about a minute and a half.

"Checkmate," he replied.

Ellison smiled big.

"What the hell happened," said Dave as he resurfaced with a cup of tea, the strings from the bags hanging from the lid. "Take it easy on him, Ted."

"Dave, you forget what it was like to be a beginner. It'll take longer to learn how to take the offensive if you don't learn how to defend yourself."

"He's right," said Dave.

"Play again?" said Ted.

"Absolutely," said Ellison immediately.

The same thing happened the next game, then the game after that.

"I appreciate you taking the time, but I'm sure Dave would like to play."

"Actually, I don't mind. I'll beat him next week."

Dave smiled at Ted.

"We have to go in ten minutes, so our wives can go to the movies," said Ted. "Are you moving on, or staying here a while?"

Ellison thought it was interesting how he phrased the question.

"Moving on."

"Well, let's have at it again."

Ted looked at Dave.

"Did you read it?"

"Yes. You were right," replied Dave.

Ellison knew the questions were personal, and focused on his part. This time Ted repeated his strategy, and Ellison was more prepared. It took almost 7 minutes for Ted to beat him.

"Much better that time. You pick up fast."

"Thank you."

Ted and Dave got up, and put the pieces into the box, every piece its own place, the weight of the wood box certain and sure. Ellison stood, too.

"So is there someone who Ted can't beat?" he said to Dave.

"Yes. But we don't talk about it." Dave smiled ear to ear at Ted.

Ted hung his head slightly in defiance at Dave, then turned to Ellison.

"We have a friend from college named Shane Purdue. He's a very frustrating anomaly when it comes to chess."

"Doesn't practice. Kicks the shit out of Ted," said Dave.

Ted injected.

"He's like Napoleon to war."

"He's a savant?" said Ellison, as if the gift were beyond explaining.

"No. He's unpredictable. Logic and emotions all wrapped into one. A contradiction in a game of strategy," Ted's tone was as if waving a white flag.

Ellison offered his hand to each of them.

"I'm Ellison. Thanks again."

"We know," said Dave with an assured smile.

"Pleasure was ours," said Ted as they left.

Ellison watched them go, feeling he'd made true friends that he would never see again. He respected them for keeping his identity out of their exchange. He stood feeling lonely, and with an anxious purpose. He smiled at himself.

I want more chess. What a beautiful distraction.

He sat back in Ted's chair, looking out at the tree line above the building and homes in the distance.

Dear Rowdy,

I know you have so much to live up to. (BTW, have you thanked your parents recently for your name?).

Thanks for the WHOLE Battlestar Galactica series on DVD for my birthday. I know I thanked you once, but wanted you to know that all the hours with the "tube" alienated the Mrs. perfectly. So, mission accomplished. (Of course she wouldn't watch it with me, so it couldn't make a difference. Divorce is inevitable).

Don't say anything to the guys yet, o.k.?

I thought of this last night, but the time wasn't right. You know how everyone on Galactica sleeps with each other indiscriminately? Nothing to do but fight and "frack." I mean, who couldn't love Starbuck, or Six, right? My point is, these people aren't real. But the Galactica is Hollywood - a backdrop for a superficial fuck-fest (excuse my "French" and prudishness) that we accept because we wish our lives could be so exciting and new. But it's not real.

I'm not even real anymore. How could I be?

The fact of the matter is, sex screws us up by mistaking it for LOVE; that's how she caught me. And for guys, it's always good. Even if we can take sex out of the equation to find the right woman, sooner or later she changes or you change, and what's left is what's real.

She says she doesn't love me anymore. That's bullshit. She never did. You know how I know? Because I'm happy living a normal life with her and she isn't.

So I've pretended she was never ready to leave Galactica, so to speak, and that's why she can't face the fact that our life wasn't real. So she can get back out there and play this fucking game again.

I thought I was old enough to make the right decision. I hope you find what and who you're looking for...
Your friend,
Shane

Chapter Six
Diversion

Bremerton had such a hometown, rural feel to it that Ellison imagined a time when it was small, with the same lush, green vegetation. He admired how the homes were built among the trees, as if none were cut during construction. The town rose up away from the water to a crest of trees and ample roof tops. He knew it dipped down toward the highway. It would certainly be a terrific workout to bicycle up and down the hills and highways along this part of the peninsula.

His brain scanned the area and imagined what would satisfy his curiosity, now peaked.

A bookstore, of course.

He entered the cafe and asked a girl if there was somewhere to find books in Bremerton.

She gave him directions, which were quite simple. He mounted his motorcycle, and arrived at a local store within minutes. He found the hobby section, and flipped through several chess books with diagrams and lessons, and decided on one. He suddenly realized that he was creating a problem and hadn't thought things through. Not only did he not have a chess game, but where was he going to put the board on a bike?

"Is there a hobby shop to buy a chess game around here?" he asked the guy at the register.

"Let's see. There's a strip mall here with a hobby shop. It's next to a Subway and a cigar store, down the street from the movie theater."

Ellison put his new book in his saddlebag and headed to the hobby shop just fifteen minutes before closing. He was surprised how many sets he had to choose from. There were marble sets, and wood sets, then plastic and metal. There was a renaissance style, and Lord of the Rings style, and gothic and plain styles. He liked the classic style made of wood, hand carved with a delicate, authentic finish.

"May I see this set, please?" he said to the store keeper, an older man with a beard, possibly the owner.

"Sure." He opened the glass case and slid the set between two others, the glass shelf above. They walked to the counter so Ellison could inspect it. He picked up the box first, 12 x 12 inches and 3 high, lifted the lid, and took a deep breath through his nostrils.

"Umm. Smells wonderful."

"It's cedar," said the store keeper.

He then inspected the pieces; the castle, then the king with the standard cross on top, easy to differentiate from the queen. He didn't like guessing between them and the queen with her bishops.

This set is perfect.

"Damn," he muttered under his breath, barely audible.

"What's wrong? You don't like something about it?" said the bearded man.

"No. Just the opposite. It's just what I wanted."

The man smiled and then tilted his head to one side, raising his shoulders.

"The problem is, I don't have room for it in my bags on the motorcycle."

"Oh."

The bearded man looked immediately past Ellison to the wall behind him.

"I think I can solve your problem. Do you like leather or canvas?"

He followed the man's attention to several backpack-like bags hanging on pegs. They weren't made for bikes, but the styles complimented his saddlebags, especially the green canvas. He could actually close each strap inside the two bags, and the weight of the cedar box would rest on the license plate holder.

"Genius," stated Ellison to the store keeper, beaming from ear to ear.

"Well, we aim to please."

He paid the man and thanked him again upon exiting. He rested his treasures on the seat of the bike and took great pleasure with the snug fit the game slid into the canvas bag. He then tested it on the back of his bike. He shook his head at just how marvelous the whole thing came together.

Ellison spent the rest of the night, secluded in his motel room playing with the game like a child at Christmas with a new toy. He went from page to page of the book, and it began coming together what Ted had meant about the basics. Of course, book knowledge was one thing, and playing a live person was another.

He fell asleep around 11 pm.

The next morning, he awoke early. The past evening was so close to him, and he felt guilty about the diversion. Perhaps this was the first time in his life he experienced self-exiled loneliness, but his contentment the previous day made him uncomfortable, and it had to end and end now. He only snacked on the continental breakfast downstairs before rolling out. He needed to feel the road beneath him, and clear his mind from what he now considered nonsensical details.

Ellison found a post office, and sent the canvas bag with chess game, and book to Colorado on the way to the highway...

Chapter Seven
Anomaly

Amos awoke with eager anticipation. The day was going to be a new adventure, a freedom he hadn't felt in quite a while. He rolled off the bunk onto his feet like a hero jumping into determined action across from Dawson City at the River Hostel. After a self-made shower, cup of coffee and donut at the Cyber Cafe, he set out on a hike up above the town. He viewed the cemeteries from the past the day before, but had been distracted. Today he melted into the history, pretending it bore little difference for him and those 110 years ago. However life then was a different exercise of will and physical demands. This day was by choice.

The altitude was easy on his lungs. A story was working out its details in his mind, and this climate and air was an aphrodisiac to his imagination. He wondered whether this bombardment of ideas hit other writers so forcefully at 26.

"Eat your heart out Hollywood," he thought at the crest of a mountain plateau.

Amos stopped to admire the view, and felt like he could fly on sheer willpower. There was no way to describe the trees in three dimension, the way they gave glimpses of the town below; a town out of history, kept authentic as possible under the circumstances. He'd been dreaming about this for 2 years. It was one thing to be young, another for youth and intellect to be compounded by experience. It was experience he needed. Just ten years ago, Amos' mind prevented sleep 'til all hours of the night due to its frivolous activity and scenarios.

He was back by 1 pm, sitting on the bunk jotting plot lines into a notebook. He was too wound up, took another shower, colder then the last, and hung out at the cafe until his 3:30 rendezvous appeared.

Their eyes met in synchronous gestures of affection, smiles communicating greater than words, touching each heart with a spurt of rhythmic flutter. Sofie came up the path from the parking area as he leaned against the wood rail of the outdoor patio at Klondike Kate's. All the tourists disappeared.

It was if their meeting was ordained by heaven in such a way, rules were necessary for lesser sorts; their love innocent.

Sofie was average female height, brownish-blond hair shoulder length. She had a beautiful oval face with expressive, brown eyes not too close together, and a smile that could disarm Amos like no one else. She wasn't the Hollywood, Sleeping Beauty, model type, but the genuine girl next door natural beauty capable of thoughtfulness, compassion, and mixed with real emotions.

She threw herself into his arms at the top of the steps; each experiencing a loss of time in the passionate throngs of a kiss so electric, the surge of energy would have revealed a disembodied spirit had one passed close enough.

A couple in their late forties sniggered as they worked their way around them and down the steps.

They finally peeled their lips apart.

"I couldn't sleep last night, thinking about today with you," she said.

"Me too, Sofie," holding her tight to his chest.

"Do you believe in love at first sight?" she said.

Amos put his right hand on her face gently, the contented smile disappearing into the warmth of her glow.

"Yes."

They kissed for another minute. She spoke first again.

"What did you say?" smiling.

He picked her up while embraced, and swung her around, legs kicking up behind her like a child swung by a father's assuring strength. She landed five feet closer to the verandah, which they entered hand in hand. They seated themselves at the back corner with the mountains high above them, ordered, and ate with their backs to everyone else, absorbed by nature. The slopes above were interrupted by ascending forests blanketing the hill. The hill overshadowed by mountains which stole their glamour to lift eyes heavenward.

Amos and Sofie ordered salads, smiling between bites. Words didn't spoil the way they gazed into each other's eyes. She stabbed a peach with her fork, offering it to him in forceful surprise. In turn he stabbed a piece of teriyaki chicken, and angled the fork so that the sauce would graze each lip. She laughed, chewing between giggles, then licked her lips clean.

Sofie was staying in the top floor of a house for several days, prearranged by friends of her parents, and they walked the dirt streets up hill in that direction. But the walk was more of a dance. They bobbed and skirted about the other like young lovers they were about to become. Three couples of seniors they passed witnessed this unpracticed choreography.

At the house, painted with bright colors and matching wood shutters, the walls, floor, and ceiling marveled and swayed with them as they basked and languished together in perfect harmony the next 16 hours; like a honeymoon, it was their first time. Three times they awoke throughout the night, and two times he used his gift of massage to assure her of her importance. He was sensitive, and asked her questions, and they treasured each other as if nothing else mattered. The real world didn't exist. There was no one to judge them, or ask for permission.

Sofie left the next morning. They washed their faces in the other's tears, despite plans and promises made. If time proved their love true, then the circumstances of life would be the story teller.

Chapter Eight
Good Measures

Ellison spent the next 2 days on the peninsula, stopped in Port Townsend and Sequim for the night. He ate lobster at the 3 Crabs Restaurant on the Dungeness Spit, and drove the mountain back roads of the "banana belt" before heading to Port Angeles. He cataloged the sights and sounds, but it was void of emotion, and he realized that these well laid plans weren't what he truly needed. He needed departure from the norm; unpredictability. It was the uncertainty of the water's spray aboard the ferry to Victoria, Canada that finally released the tension he'd felt since Bremerton. Somewhere between the cheap motels and the roadside lunches of the Alaskan Highway, Ellison began to feel right about himself and his tortured existence again.

The highway wasn't cut through the tall trees along the way, as expected. It must have taken years of planning to build bridge after bridge to cross an equal number of river crossings. Very few times was he lost among the trees, or walls of forests aligning each side. The highway disappeared in the distance, a point he was continually chasing, and that was his main concern. The view he witnessed was one incredible nuance after another, and it was the mountains that dominated landscapes, not the trees. Only had the trees come alive, as in fantasy books, would it be easy to imagine how completely one would be swallowed up.

From Victoria, Vancouver Island, and the renewal of his soul, he ate up the scenery like a baby at a mother's breast; most sacred and profound. Then totally out of place was Prince George, British Columbia. The countryside was lovely, but off the highway the city was beaten down by harsh winters, and like a dingy American downtown.

The main goal of the journey was Dawson City, Yukon Territory, and then Alaska. But the high point wasn't just arriving. He stayed in Dawson Creek, and tackled the most obscure part of the route into the Northern Territory the next day, taking mental note of

Charlie Lake and the overall feel of community in this area just by the way the lay of the land and homes sprawled across the countryside.

Between there and Chetwynd, several times Ellison had to stop along the road and weep. The way the river wound along the highway, twisting and opening up to banks of dirt, bends, and upcroppings of terrace-like fields of grass, all the while encased by the 'university of trees,' as it were, was hard to imagine just a coincidence and randomness of nature.

It was so easy to imagine homesteading there. This was the case too, and it teleported him back to a time where family was the ultimate means of survival, and reminiscent of a happy hearth. The placement of dominant mountains, lusciously forested and green, acted like a maze of centurions to be navigated around and a test for the worthy. The beauty was so overwhelming and exquisite, he put himself in a vulnerable position just by being there, and one he unconsciously expected.

Chetwynd was quaint, small and had an artsy feel with wood carvings decorating the highway through town. It had a huge water tank overlooking the residents like Boulder City, NV, on route to Hoover Dam. The sign in town was a wood post, engraved with "Chetwynd" like the marking of a ranch, with a grizzly bear carving underneath, and leaving town yet another sign with "British Columbia" added to the name of the town with an array of flowers around the base. Ellison imagined living there.

Beyond these mountains the obscurity of the north began to be more apparent. Several times he slowed down suddenly to wait for buffalo herds to cross the two lane highway ahead. His senses came alive as he passed, heart beating heavily in his chest while watching for the dominant male and imagining the worst. The noise of his bike was a great ally. Once he saw a black bear along the tree line, and beeped his horn to warn the animal.

He stopped to look out at yet another lake that defied description, the services of some local shop unnecessary to him. Ellison had lost count of the times he crossed a river along the way, and imagined how difficult it would be in frontier days to navigate through this intense wilderness. That was why the Pacific Ocean route by boat was the only way in the days of the gold rush.

The Alaskan Highway zigzagged along the British Columbia border running east/west until finally committing itself to the

Northwest Territory. Ellison made another mental note of Lake Watson city proper, the first town inside the Territory, and an old sign that marked the miles to places across North America and the world. This reaffirmed how he was living free with the country on his bike, sometimes uneasily. Traveling these roads was too dangerous on motorcycle at night. Cars and trucks often hit deer or antelope or moose who cross the road.

Kathy's Kitchen with a subtitle on the sign "A Little Taste of Home" was a delightful place to have lunch. He ordered, and then retreated to a picnic table outside on the deck, enjoying the escape from his helmet, yet hiding behind his baseball cap. He wished he'd found a hat less confining and stereotypical, something like Gilligan's, a fishing hat, or Navy cap. The miles sign marked the actual lake was 8 miles away, and just 322 miles to his first important milestone, historic Whitehorse, Yukon Territory. He appreciated that this sign was in miles rather than kilometers like all the other posts since crossing the border into Canada.

Appealing to tourists from the states.

His heart leaped inside his chest in anticipation, but Whitehorse would have to wait. There was no way he could make it before sunset.

He was extremely lucky to escape any rain this part of the trip. Rain wasn't only uncommon in the summertime, it was expected. He stayed at the lakeside Yukon Motel & Restaurant, in Teslin, 173 miles north of Lake Watson, leisurely taking pictures of the fireweed along banks obscured by tall grass and almost prairie-like shorelines. The bridge over the lake was an expansive multi-parker through truss with white painted steel, and the reflection on the still water was quite picturesque.

He wasn't hungry, so after getting a room, Ellison got a delicious cup of coffee and strolled out onto the end of the dock on the lake, admiring the sun as it lit up the haze of the horizon, tree speckled mountains in the distance. He didn't notice several couples coming his way until their footsteps reverberated on the man-made dock. He looked back suddenly with nowhere to go.

They were all in their late sixties, and one lady was looking from a postcard to the view that mirrored its picture in her hand.

"Hello, there. Hope we're not disturbing you?" one of the men said.

"Of course not," he lied, not selfishly.

"Would you take our picture since we have you trapped?" said the other lady.

Ellison smiled at her obvious humor.

"Sure."

They cautiously stepped to the edge of the dock to allow him to go around them after taking two shots with the shore and motel in the background. Then he took two pictures of the bridge and lake as a backdrop.

"Hey. Don't I know you," said the other man suddenly. "Aren't you the fellow who owns a real estate agency in Edmonton?"

"You're from Canada?" he replied.

"Of course. This is our back yard. It just took sixty something years to get here," he joked.

Ellison laughed.

"No. I'm a bloody Yank, I'm afraid," he responded.

"Well. Enjoy your travails," said the man using the last word ironically.

Ellison was up early, as usual, and quite admittedly enjoyed the fresh bakery in the restaurant. He packed his bike, and roared off toward the north. There was little traffic that morning, and he slowed to 40 miles per hour so he could take in a mountain range he had never seen the likes of. The tree line was so thick, it looked like an inexperienced artist's rendering. To him the mountains range had a thick nineteen century beard from base to mid-mountain.

The motorcycle began descending from above a plateau. Suddenly the wonderfully bluish-black Yukon River emerged, and Whitehorse, Yukon Territory. Ellison drove over the bridge next to the authentically preserved SS Klondike paddle boat. The level high ground on each side of the historic portion of town gave a feel of coziness and smallness, as demonstrated by the fact that everything was reachable by foot. The Nissan car dealership's inventory was extremely small, and parking was more than adequate for the local stores and restaurants.

He drove the circumference of the town clockwise to get a lay of the landmarks. The local radio station had a large banner called "The Rush," referencing the origin of Whitehorse as the entry point to the gold rush of the late 1800s. He drove down 1 Avenue which paralleled the river, location of the tourist information center, local government buildings, and museums. He turned into the Canada Best

Value Inn Motel on the corner of Wood Street, just two blocks north of Main, and across from the MacBride Museum.

Fortunately they had a room open for the two nights he'd planned on staying, and off the lobby was a Korean Restaurant open for the tourist season. The room was perfect, a second bed to lay out his clothes, a shelf to set his saddlebags directly inside the door below a hanging rack, its own coffee machine, and a large window with thick curtains. He immediately closed the drapes for privacy; the rear of the building had a cement slab patio above the room. He was also delighted the facility had its own laundry machines in the basement, a long ramp leading to the stairs.

There was a Starbucks on Main & 2nd and he was looking forward to his usual cup of Pike's Place blend in the morning. He got the busy work over, and laid his freshly clean clothes out on the spare bed. He wouldn't pack his saddlebags 'til the 2nd morning, and hung a dress shirt out for dinner.

Ellison walked 1st Avenue to Main. He ordered a sandwich and ice tea at the Baked: Cafe & Bakery adjacent to souvenir shops, which were understandably prominent in town. The cafe was crowded, fresh smelling and jubilant with conversation, obviously a local hang out.

"I wonder if they have a fishing hat," he thought under the baseball cap.

The hallway between the cafe and shops was like an indoor mini-mall, with several businesses at the back. He found everything but what he wanted; plates and cups with moose decor, dream catchers, wood and ceramic statues of animals, postcards, t-shirts, sweatshirts, and ironically, chess sets of every kind.

There would be time to look elsewhere tomorrow. He walked the long way down 2nd Avenue back to the motel, the sky gray with low clouds. Laid out across the bed, Ellison took an unexpected nap. Awaking several hours later, he didn't know what to do with himself. He wasn't hungry, and didn't feel like going out. He settled on the television, flicking the channels ungratifyingly, unable to decide on what to watch.

If only I could read Sea Wolf.

He reassured himself that waiting for Dawson was the right choice.

Ellison clicked through channels 'til the top of the hour and settled on a documentary that extraterrestrials settled Earth, prompting more questions than it answered. It was disappointing to say the least. A year ago he watched a documentary which informed him of a discovery that changed how he perceived the universe, as he was sure it did the whole scientific community; that black holes are at the center of every galaxy. He was mystified. He loved science and marveled about space since a kid. Carl Sagan's Cosmos which aired on PBS intensified it. Whether there was any truth to the whole E.T. on Earth thing, it remained to be seen.

The days had run into one another since leaving Colorado, and Ellison had to think hard what day it was in relation to the working world around him as he hit the sidewalk at 6:30 am. It was a Thursday and Starbucks was a welcome routine he missed. He was looking forward to visiting the SS Klondike, and was in no hurry because of the early hour, despite the fact that the book in his hand was not his first choice. This was the dilemma.

When he packed the books he wanted to bring, he had no desire to read his "normal" choices of topics; which were what he considered his usual intellectual "long haired" stuff. Instead he brought "Replay" by Ken Grimwood, a novel with good possibilities a fan had sent him, and of course "The Sea Wolf." It was also the only London book he hadn't read that he really wanted to.

Ellison didn't feel like starting Replay. He'd already started Sea Wolf. But this was part of the healing process, getting his mind off of it, and the only other book he'd grabbed off his bookcase at home was William Blake's "Songs of Innocence and of Experience." So there he sat in the corner next to the front window under his hat reading poetry.

The copy had facsimiles of Blake's own art and handwritten words in full color, and the printed poems on the next page which was more readable. He got to the 13th page, "The Little Lost Boy," before his anxiety peaked. The next poem was "The Little Boy Found," by his mother no less, which he took offense at the implication that the father was so irresponsible, that he would allow him to wander into the elements in the first place.

Certainly, poetry requires a sense of "looking inward" to begin with, but the fact that modern society depicts women as the primary caregiver, especially in case of divorce, was a stereotype. One in which Blake was portraying as well several hundred years earlier.

A friend of Ellison had his heart broken in court because of this favoritism. The court had reinforced his despair, despite the fact that he was a better parent, and had given no reason for the bias. After 2 years of beating himself up, he'd committed suicide after the indoctrination of his Ex-wife had made his young children turn on him. Next to his suicide note was a check for over $100,000.

Is this all a father was, a child support payment?

His face swelled up at his own loss, and Ellison put the book down on the table.

Enough poetry for one day.

He put it out of his mind as a rugged looking man entered Starbucks with a brown cowboy hat. He held the door for a woman passing him the opposite direction pulling a sweet, little girl wearing pink leggings. They looked like little sticks attached to a giant red coat with fake, white fur around her collar. The sight was befitting his thoughts.

He looked at his watch. Only 7:46. He grabbed the book, exhaling instinctively, and left. The morning fog was lifting enough to reveal a sliver of blue sky above the plateau on the east, and passing a bank on the corner he noticed the temperature on its sign was a balmy 56 degrees.

"Not bad for a summer day," he thought sarcastically.

He admired a large tent community of summer travelers right off 1 Avenue in Rotary Park, next to the road and Lewes Blvd. which was a bridge that scaled the Yukon River.

You couldn't get away with that in the United States, especially without paying for it.

The road forked and he walked along the S Access Rd. to the massive passenger boat on the bank of the river, brightly painted white with paddles a bright orange, equally spanning the width of the boat to the deck. The plateau on the west behind the SS Klondike was forested by trees that cleared the ledge. But the shore was barren, mostly rocks and sand compared to the southeast shoreline which was like the opposite plateau. Schools and hotels overlooked the river to the east, and behind them the mountains Ellison descended the day before.

A huge barge sat behind it with fading red paint and housed a large white tent where the tour apparently began. The impression the ship had once pulled it was unmistakable. He didn't wait the hour before it opened, and walked around the incredible sight imagining that its weight must have displaced a huge amount of water. Little did Ellison know just how big the Yukon River would become upstream traveling north to Dawson City, and the entire width of Alaska to the Bering Sea.

The Klondike was surrounded by a beautiful grass park which was next to a round-a-bout. In the middle, Ellison got a thrill from the Canadian flag and sign. Usually he took jet airplanes to foreign countries. But people from the United States take Canada for granted, more than Canada does of the U.S. He smiled big at "The Rush" sign he passed again walking back into town on 4th Avenue.

The air of the town was different from others that same size he'd experienced. He imagined it was the fact his brain knew he was on the edge of the world, obscured so far north, and on the border of society. He felt a sense of security those who lived here a hundred years ago did not.

Ellison walked past a house zoned for a small business painted bright blue, a white picket fence around it, a grassy yard, and the most gorgeous blue flower bush which matched the color of the house.

I wonder what it's called?

The shops were beginning to open and he spent an hour wandering around town, still unable to find the hat he wanted. He had a piece of fudge in a store on Main, admittedly not the most nutritious breakfast. He also bought a t-shirt with an accurate map of the Yukon Territory and points of interest along the way to Anchorage, Alaska. To his great surprise, Ellison found another book to read, perfect for his predicament at the most unexpected place; a drug store on Main and 3rd Avenue. The book, short stories by Anton Chekhov.

Ironic that as Ellison's real life was filled with a desire to avoid living people around him, as he poured through the stories by Chekhov, the experience on the page reconnected him to humanity, love, relationship, loyalty, betrayal, all the nuances of youth, first love, and the simple connections to the world that is often lost because of modern technology. Some of the stories he read left him shaking his head at the abrupt ending, with no conclusion other than the imaginings of his own mind. He found a particular fascination and longing to the story "A Living Chattel."

It was 7:37 pm, and he set the book on his table at the Edgewater Hotel Restaurant looking around at people, and feeling a new connection inspired by the stories. The room was decorated with real wood, a step up dining area where Ellison sat, and polished wood spindles, corner posts, and half wall dividers separating the room into a positive atmosphere to sit and socialize.

He hadn't been to his motel since that morning, but felt like injecting himself into a real conversation. This scared him immensely. The thought of Sylvester Stallone's character in the last "Rocky Balboa" movie flashed in his mind, where Rocky mingled with the patrons at his restaurant, moving from table to table, telling reminiscing stories of glory days.

"That's just not going to happen," he thought laughing at himself.

Just then, the waitress interrupted him.

"Sir, are you having dinner tonight?"

An empty glass of beer shone like a beacon on the table, and in Ellison's mind it screamed an obvious lack of etiquette.

"I'm not sure..." he said looking around.

"Well if you'd like a refill, I can sit you at the bar. But we need the table if you're not eating."

The hotel was on Main across from the bakery. It had a giant "E" calligraphy style sign in green and gold on the corner of 2nd, and the exterior was brown and off-white with board and batten wood like an authentic pub on the British Isles. He looked over at people waiting to be seated at the entrance.

"No, thank you. I'll be staying. But I'm not a bar person."

He smiled as she handed him the menu, but felt totally stupid about what he'd said.

What the hell does that mean, Ellison?

"I hope that didn't sound snobby," looking up into her youthful eyes.

"No, of course not."

Her tone wasn't convincing at all. From his short experience in Whitehorse, he'd learned that the majority of help in town were seasonal, from other parts of Canada, and the girls he'd met that day seemed to lack experience in customer service. They weren't rude; they just had a matter of fact attitude like someone on the phone with a long distance carrier, if there was such a thing anymore.

The young woman sat two couples at the table next to him as he decided what to order. They were in their 30s and obviously Canadian by the use of the expression, "nice place, aye." One of the men nodded his direction.

Ellison forced a smile and responded with "how are you folks?" Rocky Balboa's image flashed in his head again. He realized his baseball cap was on indoors, and set it on the table.

It was impossible to ignore them, the tables were so close. They were on vacation and had just returned from Dawson City.

"What's the weather like there?"

A man in a gray t-shirt depicting a screaming family driving over the Top Of The World Highway answered, sitting across from him next to his wife.

"Really perfect. It has been raining coming out of Alaska. The dirt roads were really muddy around Chicken, but it stopped our first day in Dawson."

"I'm sorry. Chicken?"

He must have said something naive because they all laughed.

"I'm sorry. We're not laughing at you," said the man's wife.

Was the look on my face that bad?

"Chicken was a mining camp during the gold rush and it's really in the middle of nowhere. Sort of the whole appeal. The miners wanted to call it ptarmigan," the woman's pronunciation of the word formed a question, "after the local bird about the same size as a chicken, but they didn't know how to spell it. So they named it Chicken."

She turned to her husband with a huge smile, "how do you spell 'ptarmigan?'"

"Heck if know," he said with a big shrug like the answer wasn't important.

"It is really cool," said the other woman, the word 'cool' showed a distinct accent.

"Are you heading into Alaska, too?" said the man wearing the t-shirt?"

"Yeah. Eventually," Ellison replied.

"I'm Hank," he said, and then he introduced his wife Helen, and their friends Mike and Padme.

"Nice to meet you," he said.

Padme, of India descent, sitting next to him offered her hand and a big beautiful smile.

"I'm Ellison. Nice to make your acquaintance," accompanied a real smile.

The waitress appeared out of nowhere standing above him.

"Are you ready to order, sir?"

"Sure. I'll have the steak," pointing to the menu.

When Ellison was distracted, Hank put his hand up to his mouth at a right angle, and mouthed something to Mike. Padme leaned in to understand, but Helen wasn't privy to his message, so he then leaned into his wife's ear underneath her blond hair as he whispered.

"No. I think I'll have an ice tea with that, thank you."

The waitress then turned her attention to the two couples...

Ellison waited for the new acquaintances to speak next, in which they did. Hank volunteered information about where they were from in Canada.

"America's a big place, especially when driving," said Ellison trying to avoid his residence as the topic. It had the opposite effect.

"We're not the ones who like to be called Americans," said Hank.

"I assumed there would be no real distinction. It's easier than being called," he paused, "United Statesian."

They laughed.

"That's true," said Helen, looking toward her husband for approval.

"You don't think you're better, a citizen of the U.S.?" asked Padme with a naive hint of aggression. Her husband Mike, jumped in before looking at Ellison's expression.

"Honey. I think you're reading too much into what you hear on the news."

"Tell that to your family. They didn't exactly value your cousin's opinion when he voted for President Obama."

"They're from Minnesota," he told Ellison, "and what we say and what we do are different sometimes, especially when family visits for Thanksgiving." The latter part was directed to his wife.

"I don't see the difference," Padme replied.

She was obviously first generation Canadian, and her custom was to be perfectly blunt, as if the social graces were yet unlearned and

40

unimportant. Her inherent beauty made allowances for her frank attitude. Mike was about to reply when Ellison interjected.

"If I might," his hand up to stop the response already formed on his lips.

"She's right, of course. The U.S. comes across as the moral superiority, especially to other countries. Sometimes it's reinforced by its citizens. But as far as Canada goes, I think most"... he almost said Americans, "people from the U.S. feel a kindredness. But out of necessity, Canada is very discriminating when it comes to allowing us from coming into their country for their own good, even more so, since the economy went downhill. Each government looks out for its own interests."

"What do you mean discriminating? That's racist!" she said.

"It doesn't imply racism, Padme. The word also means... discerning," said her husband.

"I know what may help," said Ellison. "Have you heard of Joseph Campbell, Padme?"

She shook her head no.

"Campbell taught mythology for 38 years, and wrote books on how the traditions and myths of cultures reinforce our sense of meaning and purpose. He didn't feel this was something experienced in 'America.'"

Ellison made quotes with his fingers.

"It's important that we look to those archetypes in other cultures and religions to find personal fulfillment. If we did, according to Campbell, then we would realize a spiritual consciousness existed beyond what is obvious to the naked eye. In a way, you are further along than we are, generally speaking," he paused, "because you have roots to a country that is rich in intrinsic values." He looked up at the rest of them and smiled, "...beyond the whole materialism of North American society."

Padme looked at her husband.

"Wow. Don't let the Republicans hear you say that," said Helen looking from Ellison to Padme.

"Show me don't tell me," said Mike.

Ellison's philosophical explanation worked. Padme may not have understood what he was saying entirely, but what was communicated was the empathy the meaning conveyed.

"I've heard of Joseph Campbell," said Hank. "He has several documentaries on TV."

"Are you sure he plays guitar. He sounds like a teacher to me," Padme said to Mike.

Ellison blushed.

"Honey. Shh."

They all looked at Ellison and saw his reaction.

"That's okay, Padme. Looks are deceiving," he said with a big smile.

A few minutes went by in silence. Hank brought up how much he wasn't looking forward to their vacation ending so soon. He was a manager of a commercial uniform supply chain. Then the waitress showed up with Ellison's food, and he started cutting into his steak. Not long after, the two couple's food arrived, and they were all too busy to talk, other than small talk.

Ellison finished first and told the couples what a delight it was meeting them.

"Have a wonderful trip home," he said setting the tip on the table.

"Thank you. Take care," said Hank. The rest followed his lead in affirmation.

"And sorry for your loss," Mike said out of the blue.

Ellison nodded and left the bustling restaurant.

The cool air was refreshing. He walked to the hotel at peace.

Chapter Nine
Dawson City

Just when he thought he'd seen the most beautiful lakes possible, the Klondike Highway north of Whitehorse, that last 340 miles to Dawson City, proved him wrong. Laberge Lake, faintly visible as the highway veered northwest was only the introduction to Fox Lake and Little Fox Lakes beyond. Fox Lake reminded him of Lake Tahoe, and the projection of obscurity was intensified by the fact that there wasn't a boat, cabin, or soul in sight. The land took on a whole new degree of transformation.

The big landmark Ellison was looking forward to was Stewart Crossing. In between, the forests intensified and the breed of trees indigenous to the effect of perma frost spanned fields of shorter vegetation in an area where roots cannot dive deep into the ground because of the frozen land and shallow top soil. He pulled off to view a wonderful lookout only once.

Here, Amos' Sofie had passed him in her car with two hitchhikers, a young man and woman from Europe that she'd picked up near the helicopter pad on the other side of the bridge outside Dawson. When Ellison arrived at Stewart Crossing, he pulled over and laughed out loud. It consisted of a convenience store and gas pumps at the crossroads of the Stewart River bridge and the Silver Trail which led to Mayo.

But he knew the importance of this place. The Stewart River ran west into the Yukon River, and that site was where Jack London and company had their claim. He topped off his tank and continued on.

A few miles from Dawson, just before Henderson Crossing, the trees finally lined the highway as he had expected it would the whole trip. Then there it was. Ellison's heart pounded in his chest like a teenager in love for the first time. The Ellison of years gone by didn't exist here.

The RV Park & hotel, helipad, city parks with baseball diamonds, and the beautiful Klondike River as it flowed into the mighty Yukon came into view. The rock sheer opposite the Klondike marked the entrance. The dirt mound dike began its barrier outlining the town as he turned with the road as Dawson opened up to a way of life that existed since years past, and he followed the paved road along Front Street into town 'til it ended at the ferry.

Ellison sat for a while admiring the incredible view of the river, the mountains above the west bank that began the Top of the World Highway, and every nuance that pictures could not do justice with two dimensional limitations because of its grandeur.

This made his arrival a true pleasure. Dawson City was filled with such thick atmosphere, it was easy to see its appeal in its hay day; a clearing in the thick jungle of ominous forces of nature, streets laid out in simplicity and ease in 'grid' fashion, still lined with real wood buildings and boardwalks. The scarcity of towns and people from point A to B, different degrees of obscurity that made Dawson a popular place for tourists was appropriate, and deserved.

Ellison's first goal was to check into the hotel. Doubling back, people stared at his bike as he passed the storefronts that featured the town's unique look. On the river side sat the SS Keno and the park that stretched along the dike. He read about the authentic architecture of Bombay Peggy's Inn & Pub online, turned left on Princess, and there she was on the corner of Second St. It was larger than pictures portrayed, and much prettier. Peggy's was a brothel in the gold rush days. It had been jacked up, and moved into town where it was remodeled, and added onto. It was three stories of Victorian elegance. He pulled up to the hotel entrance which was a dormer on the Second St. side, and the short width of the building.

The streets were all dirt except Front St. He parked and entered a foyer. The next door was locked. He picked up the phone on the wall, and it rang the attendant immediately.

"Hi. I'm here to check in," said Ellison cheerfully.

"Be right there," said the female voice.

A moment later, the door opened, and he entered carrying his saddlebags, taking in the impeccably lush textures of colors and furniture. The woman instructed him to move his motorcycle behind the building next to the fence of the outdoor patio. When he returned, he signed in with his card, and was instructed to remove his shoes.

There, next to the front door, was a wood shoe holder which was already half full.

"It's a real pleasure to have you here for the week. We're very discreet and want you to think of this as your home. If you need anything, please let me know. I'm Sandy the owner. My manager is Sissy, and she's usually in the pub through that door afternoons."

She pointed to a heavy wooden door down the hall. The office was under the stairs to the other floors.

"Follow me, and I'll show you to The Attic," she said with a genuine smile.

There was such a positive energy as he climbed the stairs in his socks, the plush carpet under foot. The doors to the unoccupied rooms were open. Each was equally elegant and pictures lined the walls reminding you of Peggy's past, authentic ladies in black and white dressed in period costumes, a picture of elderly Peggy on the first landing. They went down the hall, turned a corner, and then took yet another corner of stairs ascending up to the third floor. Each room had its own name, "Room Ten," "The Brigg," "The Lookout," etc.

At the end of the hall, the open door to The Attic showed the immense span of the most amazing room he'd never imagined in such a place as Dawson City. The angled roof came to a level head, dormers for windows were mere slits, and unlike the beds he passed on his way, there were two queen beds setting on a frame right on the floor in his room, one in the middle of the room on the wall which was the front of Peggy's, and the second bed was below the point of the gable on the top of the building above the hotel entrance.

Around the corner was a large flat screen TV, which he never intended to turn on. To the left of the door on the rear of the hotel, a vintage white bath tub sat inside another dormer, slender window, and sheer white curtains around the head and foot. It had its own mini-refrigerator, vanity outside the bathroom, sitting area with coffee table and wicker chairs where the front of the hotel came to another point, and a hanging rack just inside the door.

Ellison's jaw was open.

"Incredible. I never expected it to be this beautiful. Thank you," he said to Sandy, who was beaming at his reaction.

"I'm so glad you like it, Mr..."

He interrupted her.

"Please call me, Ellison"

"I will... Ellison."

Her wonderful smile continued as she backed out of the room, closing the door behind her.

Sure Ellison had stayed in hotels across the world nicer and fancier. But this was something entirely different. The Waldorf-Astoria in New York had nothing on the cozy nature of Peggy's in Dawson. He wouldn't even walk through the door if there was one here.

The Attic offered seclusion. Literally the highest point in the building, he marveled at the view out one of the windows, the Yukon River slightly obscured by the dike was just one block away. The room's appeal wasn't because of any sense of prestige, but its locale. His gear safely stowed, he marveled as he descended to the front door, put his shoes on, and walked around the corner of the building on the wood sidewalk, into the pub. They served a few h'orderves to eat, and Seth the bartender recommended The Drunken Goat, which was down the street half a block.

"They're just opening up," his hair sleeked back with an air of confidence and intelligence. He later found out Seth was a psychology major taking a break from college. Ellison looked at his watch to see that it was 5:05 pm.

The Drunken Goat was beautiful, inside and out, plants hanging and potted along the wood railing painted white and blue. Ellison sat in the bar side rather than at a table in the adjacent cafe. It was like a western saloon with a pass-through for the bartender to receive food. He had a beer, a wonderful Greek Salad, and sat taking in the amazing ambiance as if catapulted back in time. The beer was called "Midnight Sun" with a picture of a raven's wings outstretched around the sun. It was a delicious "espresso stout" from a Yukon Brewery. Ellison was not a fan of average beers, and this was a greater novelty.

By 7:00 he walked to the river and stood in awe. The Yukon was like an ominous sludge of lava as it flowed north. It bore no resemblance to the Yukon of Whitehorse. The glacier run-off made it a muddy brownish-white deluge. He looked south at where the clean Klondike River emptied into the Yukon. The blackness of the water looked like an oil spill or swarm of fish coloring the Yukon before mixing totally into a shade of whiteness, like Kahlua in a White Russian drink.

He stared at the width of the river, wondering the distance across.

A Quarter mile?

He also wondered if it would pull someone under if they fell in, and the thought scared him immensely.

Jack London's cabin was below the hill and he turned to imagine where. He would savor it tomorrow. This was also the first time it dawned on him that there would not be darkness. He forgot to even look in Whitehorse. The sun would disappear but the sky would remain lit. Above the round mountain on the other side of the river, a few tiny patchy clouds were like white puffs of smoke. The sun would set soon.

Inside Peggy's he placed his shoes on the hard wood shelf. There was a sitting area off the front door. Ellison scanned the bookcase for titles. There was a copy of London's The Call of the Wild.

Expected.

Then he noticed that management had put out two bottles of Sherry with "Peggy's" on the label, and on a crystal platter, different squares of chocolate desserts. Ellison smiled big. He lounged around in the chairs sampling both brands of wine and one piece of cake. It may have been the length of the day, or the Sherry, but he felt at peace.

Where were the other guests?

The plan was to barricade himself in his room for the rest of the night with "The Sea Wolf." Upstairs, he dropped the copy on the 2nd bed under the corner dormer, found his place and began reading.

"How I hated him! And how my hatred for him grew and grew, during that fearful time, to cyclopean dimensions. For the first time in my life I experienced the desire to murder -- 'saw red,' as some of our picturesque writers phrase it. Life in general might be sacred, but life in the particular case of Thomas Mugridge had become very profane indeed. I was frightened when I became conscious that I was seeing red, and the thought flashed through my mind: was I, too, becoming tainted by the brutality of my environment? -- I, who even in the most flagrant crimes had denied the justice and righteousness of capital punishment?" (The Sea Wolf page 66)

Ellison looked up at the sun's rays barely piercing the attic floor through the dormer window, making its way along the side of the other wall. The euphoria was so intense, he felt that nothing could take him out of the "zone." He fell into the story deeply. From time to time, looking up at the point of the roof in the room, he nodded his head side to side and smiled at how unbelievably lucky he was to be here at this moment. Only once did this feeling escape him.

If they weren't gone, I wouldn't be here. How will this change my life? Will I forget them? Will I let anyone replace them?

It was now 8:30 pm when he broke from the book with this segue of thoughtfulness. One thing was missing. He grabbed his room key, with a large brass emblem with "The Attic" on it, and made his way downstairs and three hallways to the pub.

Sweat pants, t-shirt, and no shoes were like walking around naked. He was so unaccustomed to this type of freedom around people, especially in a hotel setting where he could bump into anyone. But he was self-assured that his privacy was safe here in the eighteen hundreds. Rock 'n roll hadn't been invented yet.

He stepped through the door to the pub, slipping on a new pair of flip-flops on the cold floor, and up to a waitress at the end of the bar. The pub was full, all but one bar stool occupied with patrons stuck in a perpetual happy-hour mode.

"Hi," he said to the young woman. "Could I get some earl gray tea, please?"

"Of course," she said with a genuine smile. "I'm Sissy, by the way.

"Nice to meet you," noticing her natural beauty and curves.

He looked around the room, several people nodded at him as they engaged in conversation.

"Hello," he said politely.

Another waitress returned to the bar and put her hand on his shoulder as she stepped around him. She had an empty pitcher of beer, and two empty plates. It was necessary for her to move another pitcher to the side to fit everything.

"Excuse me, sweetie," she said, emptying her arm and hand into the plastic tub. "Are you enjoying your stay with us?"

"Immensely," Ellison replied. "I apologize for my attire."

"Oh, heavens, don't think anything of it. This is your home while here."

Sissy handed him his tea, and asked if he wanted it billed to his room.

"Yes, please," he said and handed her a Canadian dollar.

"Thank you. If there's anything else you'd like..."

"Thanks."

He turned and went back upstairs. Amos was sitting at a small table on the wall next to the piano with a pen and paper, his eyes glazed over as he watched Ellison leave, mouth hanging open. He too, left the pub, by way of the double door entrance on Princess. He stopped outside looking at the floors above, and after gaining his composure in the night air, went the direction of his bunk.

Chapter Ten
Million Micro-Computers

"Where are the mothers of these twenty and odd men of the Ghost?... There is no balance in their lives. Their masculinity, which in itself is of the brute, has been overdeveloped. The other and spiritual side of their natures has been dwarfed -- atrophied, in fact." (The Sea Wolf, page 128)

Ellison read to page 216 of 366 before putting it down. He didn't want to finish too soon, enjoying the journey so much. It would be tragic to not savor the bantering between Wolf Larsen and Humphrey, affectionately known as "Hump." He laid on the bed, looking up at the ceiling before rising, moving to the desk, and penning some words on sheets of hotel stationary. Another three quarters of an hour passed before he rose again, turned off the light, and stood looking out the window at the river. He closed his eyes and imagined the tiny town in darkness, how brilliant the stars would be. He was disappointed there was no darkness.

How dark would the town really be?

He could see a great distance from this window. Large groups of tourists walking in packs along the boardwalk.

He imagined Dawson when London was there in 1896, who would only live another 19 years to ripe age of 40. Ellison was so impressed and amazed at the diversity in The Sea Wolf. He was surprised at the philosophical debate of man as animal verses man as sentient being in the story. Surely the recognition of human attributes was the very proof Wolf Larsen refused to recognize about himself, and others, like so many today.

The ability to ask questions, form our own philosophical thoughts contriving good versus evil, and comprehend science itself, was unlike any animal on the planet; as a whole, taking our own existence for granted. And this was the beauty so thoroughly enjoyable about London's book.

Glancing skyward, he saw a light blue haze where night should be. Space travel was so easy to imagine in this obscure setting, as easy as dog sleds. He thought of the documentary in Whitehorse.

"How was the gap between primitive man and ancient man bridged?" he wondered. "Were they to become the first slaves to the 'space-gods?' Were the demigods of mythology a real step in the evolutionary ascent of man, just as science describes evolution as the ascent to modern man? How do you get from the herdsmen of Africa to Aristotle?"

Ellison recalled a wonderful conversation with a Jewish Professor from the University of Indiana a decade ago who taught Psychology. He said that "whenever a person ventures in the pursuit of truth, the level of his or her genuine desire to know what was real, determined how deep their knowledge became." His perspective of Adam and Eve verses sciences' evidence of the Earth's age reminded Ellison how truth became relative. The professor believed the story to be a type of metaphor explaining what would otherwise be unexplainable. Yet the story definitely offered a philosophical parallel which placed freewill as the first rule of God's universal laws.

"The garden trap was set," as the professor put it. "People who think predestination as an absolute don't understand human nature. A lot of these nuts think psychology is of the devil." Ellison reflected on the sarcastic remarks of Bill Maher on HBO about God as a "spaceman" fueled by his contempt for religionists. In comparison, Ellison wasn't an atheist, but looked at life as a free-for-all of scattered truth. Creationism to Ellison was our conscious choice to build a world based on ethics and reason, rather than the distraction of putting the world's responsibilities for change up to a God.

"Whether the Great Flood was 'universal' did not jeopardize faith. All it would take is an arctic glacial break."

The professor then quoted a line from one of the Star Wars movies, which was inspired by Joseph Campbell's Hero of a Thousand Faces. "Many of the truths we cling to depend greatly on our own point of view,' or even God's."

Ellison thought there was certainly intelligence across the spectrum, spanning from the primitive man to "God" as infinite; it was even an Original Star Trek episode, for heaven's sake. Who knows what was out there in the infinity of space. That didn't mean if Earth was colonized these spacemen were that different than man, other than intelligence and technology, or a superior physiological makeup; which would account for the long life spans of the Ancients in the book of Genesis. Perhaps the societies portrayed in myths were real and their progenitors lacked the understanding to articulate it. Then again, maybe the One true God did show up, Fathered a new race He would genuinely favor, and command those who were an abomination to be wiped out because their idolatry degenerated their evolution.

Some stories in mythology sounded like modern warfare described by primitive man. If there was evidence of every level of intelligence from man to a single celled organism, then it is reasonable to think intelligence could exist from the smartest man to an omniscient God.

Ellison imagined what it would be like arriving on this planet thousands of years ago, specifically Mesopotamia, and lining ships up with Ararat like the runway of a modern airport. If Earth was settled by spacemen, it wasn't his place to judge, but to perceive the possibility of different realities, like his professor friend. To Ellison it would be unethical to not look for a reasonable explanation for archeological and scientific findings.

If my fans only knew, just how un-hip I really am.

Ellison's mind drifted from topic to topic, from all its complex meandering to the amazing effort it would take to form the dike along the Yukon, until he finally dropped down on the bed under the blankets and gave himself willingly to the lord of dreams.

In it he visited a tower room where his oldest and fondest friends sat debating whether cars would one day be made of plastic, or something more ecologically safe, like woven corn husks.

He revisited from past dreams the lighthouse on the crest of a hill which changed shape to a two level home that overlooks a cliff as he nears it, and a path leading down to the water. He followed the path, but becomes trapped on a precipice that overlooks a series of natural falls like Niagara, only these have rock cliffs and vegetation growing between them like an island. How he escapes this deadly demise, completely surrounded by rushing water on both sides, is just as much a mystery as how he got there, an encompassing magnitude like a tidal wave he couldn't remember come morning.

Perhaps his subconscious cataloged all the forms his molecules previously called home, that now made up his body into his own evolution, now manifest by this one dream; the dream simply the reflection of those molecules his spirit interpreted as it changed forms through the eons of time.

Chapter Eleven
Bravado

It was quite unusual that he was able to sleep in the next morning, and even lounge around his room 'til 11. He read a few more short stories by Chekhov, and what a marvel it was to him how he complimented London's experiences, even though the geographic differences of the former existed alongside such populated cities in Russia. London's knack was putting humanity on the edge of nature to see how man reacted to it.

Ellison was kindred to the creative aspect which reflects the mind's eye, inspiring those who experienced this vicariously through his music. It never dawned on him that though he was a pupil to the classic writers of the past, he made more money than they ever dreamed of because of the technology of the media. He was aware that if they wrote in modern times in the styles which made them so unique and prolific, a modern agent or publisher would reject those works; Faulkner specifically came to mind. It wasn't because of the general public's inability to comprehend them, but the business that perceived that they couldn't, and in order to reach 21st century readers, they had to dumb down material or stick to a format that was somewhat predictable. Dan Brown's "DiVinci Code" was the book that came to Ellison's mind as he readied himself to go out.

He slipped out the wood and screen door at the end of the hall on the third floor, putting on a different pair of shoes on the landing of the outside stairs on the east side alley facing the mountains. He took Second St. south to Church, then left up the hill, admiring the artistic construction of a house apropos to the time with a shake accent dormer painted a bright green-blue that flowed throughout the rest of the trim around the house, and contrasting olive green along the sidewalks of horizontal boards on the second floor, and vertical along the first and ground level patio on the front of the home.

The town ended on Eight St. He turned right, the dust of the dirt road building on his 3/4" top brown hiking shoes. Robert Service's Cabin was visible immediately. Its existence completely escaped

Ellison. He'd forgotten who he was as well. Later that day he saw his book of poetry, feeling stupid to forget such a prominent author who penned the famous "Cremation of Sam McGee."

At the end of the street as it curved into Firth, a replica of Jack London's log cabin made from the original logs helped Ellison along the journey in time. He was lost in his imagination, healed by a peaceful time experienced from youth, as he had visited this place and others in "The Call of the Wild," and "White Fang." A sign hung near the corner, "Jack London Square." A fellow tourist, a young woman, commented how lucky they were to live in the modern world as he approached. The young man with her stood taking a picture before they left.

The 'new world' takes its history for granted. How much of it will be lost in future generations?

He focused his mind back in time, and smiled to himself. He went through the white picket fence surrounding the site. The cabin was incredibly small, void of privacy inside. His hand ran along the wood of the old walls, the size of it the most humble circumstance. The true amenity of its time was the roof over their heads and the stove to warm them. He learned more than he had known from the guide inside the much larger museum, photos and articles along its walls, and miraculously, a picture of London at 21 after arriving in camp. He learned that he spent a short time at the cabin, located 75 miles south of Dawson, and a shorter time recuperating from Scurvy in the town, the harshness of life at sea already taking its toll on his nutritionally depleted body. Ellison was amazed at just how serious this trip had been to him, yet he inspired so many for ages to come.

The cache, as it was called, a small building on stilts between the two buildings, was used to keep food from bears and other animals. Ellison held the gate open for a large crowd of senior citizen tourists arriving as he left. He walked to the Museum with a collection of narrow-gauge locomotives, and then Fourth St. to King and Klondike Kate's for lunch.

There wasn't a second to spare. He had dreamed about it his whole life or half of it anyway. Amos had sent Ellison two books through the mail by authors he thought would interest him, and hoped this would be remembered. And then, there were the right poems to choose of his own, the chapter from a story he had rewritten, and most of all, the synopsis for the story all worked out in his head named after one of Ellison's songs.

After he had compiled everything, he rushed it down to Bombay Peggy's and left it with the desk in the yellow envelope. When he returned he checked out of his bunk, and into a spot to pitch his tent. He relaxed back and imagined Ellison finding the work with the note attached.

"...I am such a big fan. Your work has changed my life, and been an inspiration... I look forward to speaking with you, and getting your input. Sincerely, Amos."

Amos felt new again after the extra trip across the Yukon on the ferry. The short night was catching up to him, especially after the previous night with Sofie, and now he checked the time frequently. He wanted to run into Ellison that night, but wondered how to do so smoothly and without embarrassing him.

A good hour later, the sun had warmed the spot where Ellison sat quietly at the gazebo at the park on Front St., and he paralleled the Yukon on his way back to the hotel to retrieve his book. Upon return to the gazebo, other tourists, mainly unkempt young travelers from Europe, had invaded this scenic spot, so he made his way to another area along a gravel trail. It gave him a better view of both rivers, so he accepted this location to pick up where he left off.

Ten minutes into The Sea Wolf he reached for his bottled water. When he went to set it back down, the slope of the hill took it, and he hopped to his feet to rescue it from the Yukon River. His foot caught soft dirt, sliding downhill, and the book which was in his left hand skirted the incline as his arm flew behind his back as a counterweight, just enough to be knocked free. It cart wheeled down the gravel slope spine over end, corner after corner, disappearing into what appeared to be the liquid concrete below of the Yukon, along with the bottle.

"No!" he shouted mortified, his mouth was open in disbelief.

The scene immediately got caught in a memory loop in his head, replaying over and over again as he was unable to stop the situation, and unable to grasp the fact that it happened.

He stood looking at the embankment down river, but couldn't even glimpse the book. The irony of The Sea Wolf being set free was both absurd, and far from laughable. It took another minute of complete denial before Ellison could consider moving on. Bewildered, he turned toward the small town. All of a sudden his mission had dramatically changed. He was not leaving Dawson City without finishing that book, and so he set out to find a replacement.

For the rest of the afternoon, he spent his time trying to reacquire what simply wasn't available, even at the library. What shops did sell Jack London's books only carried "White Fang" & "The Call of the Wild," and other stories from the Yukon.

Maximillian's Gold Rush Emporium, Dawson Trading Post with antique hard cover books, the gift shop at the monstrous Westmark Inn, where he saw Service's poetry, was all void of London's sea voyage. Ellison even took the ferry to the River Hostel, at the suggestion of a clerk, who said the owner may have a copy in his gift shop or the recreation room. He was too stressed to enjoy this first voyage on the Ferry, meant to be savored another day. The rec room was hopeful. The entire rear wall housed shelves of books, but no Sea Wolf.

By the time Ellison returned to Bombay Peggy's, he was admittedly in a foul mood. Not only did he not make eye contact with anyone, but he didn't even reply to the desk clerk who handed him the manila envelope with Amos' work. He threw it onto the wicker chair as he flopped down onto the bed, staring off into space above without even seeing the white paint, 2x4 studs in the truss, or imagined shingles on the roof. Only the book tumbling into the river.

Ellison shook his head in disbelief again. He had 66 pages left to read. Humphrey and Maude had just taken on the seals for their skins, and Humphrey had woken to find the Ghost on the beach of Endeavor Island.

What she was doing there? What threat awaited them?

Ellison didn't know simply because he reached for a drink of water.

"Damn," muttered Ellison.

He sat up, and looked around the room.

Will I have to drive to Alaska before finishing?

It didn't seem right to him.

"Damn it," he complained again aloud.

He needed to calm his nerves. He picked up the house phone, and asked for a cup of tea. The girl asked if he wanted it brought to his room.

"That would be perfect. Thank you."

He looked over at the yellow envelope, retrieved it, and pulled out its contents. Ellison read the note, and threw the packet down on the table.

Great. That's all I need.

Ellison opened the door to the room, and began pacing back and forth. He didn't realize that though he attempted to rid his life of attachment, he had now fallen into a distraction that had completely consumed him. Suddenly, he realized that he had forgotten why he was there to begin with, and the isolation from those he truly loved hit him. He walked slowly to the door, closed it, and fell down next to the bed sobbing.

A few minutes passed before a knock permeated the silence. Ellison got to his feet, wiped his face, and answered the door.

"Here's your tea, sir," said Amos.

Ellison took it and set it on the coffee table, returning with a dollar, not even looking into Amos' face.

"I don't want your money, sir. I'm Amos. I'm doing them a favor downstairs."

"Thank you very much. I appreciate it."

He closed the door as Amos stood expecting something entirely different. Amos smiled to himself and worked his way downstairs in his gray socks, trying to put it all together. It finally dawned on him that Ellison didn't look at his material, or remember his name.

Hours later after the town had grown quiet, with the exception of Peggy's Pub, Ellison exited the hotel and leisurely walked south on Third St. to the Klondike River, and all the way to the Helicopter pad. The natural earth shelf just a few feet high along the bank had a perfect view as the Klondike wound around the mountain pass, opening up to 30-40 feet wide, and straightened for its final percolating song before emptying into the Yukon.

Out of sight from here, the mouth had a few tiny natural islands of shrubs. Ellison looked west to where the sun was no longer visible, but the light still furnished blue hues. It was obviously nighttime as peace filled the air in the absence of fowl. He stood for a long time while focusing on the absolute miracle of it all.

He meandered around the town with no real purpose, returned to the pub, and sat at the bar listening to conversations of other patrons. One seasonal local was the main attraction as he told stories about his travels. Two men in particular, who were part of the inner circle, listened intently. He was loud, and slightly obnoxious, but Ellison found himself smiling from time to time, and generally lost in the moment.

"Are you feeling better?" asked Sissy out of the blue, as she brought out his beer of choice.

"What makes you ask that?" he replied.

"Oh. I don't know. Your demeanor is back to normal. Besides, we try to make sure our guests are taken care of, so we keep an eye on you."

"Oh. That's just what I need," smiling.

She touched his hand empathetically and turned to work the other side of the bar.

"Were you guys really busy earlier?"

She stopped, staccato.

"No more than usual. Why?"

"You sent someone up to deliver my tea."

"Oh. That's Amos. He's been here a week, picked up a side job under the table for his trip. He said he'd be 'cool.' Was everything okay?"

"Absolutely."

Ellison finished his 2nd beer, and feeling more relaxed now, climbed the stairs to his room. The first thing he did was take a closer look at the note.

"Amos," he repeated.

Funny name. Where's he from, the South?

He took Amos' work to the bed and began ciphering through it. He reached backwards to switch on one of the small bedside lamps.

Just before ten the next morning, Amos had camped out in the pub waiting for Ellison to conveniently surface. He brought a bagel with cream cheese with him and ordered a cup of coffee. Refills were full price in the seasonal town. Then he was working on a banana he'd brought up from Whitehorse when Sissy sat down at the small table with him.

"What's up?"

"Nothing really," he replied.

"Hungry?"

He shrugged his shoulders.

"I'm a guy. I'm supposed to be an eating machine."

She smiled.

"If I didn't have a boyfriend, Amos, you'd be a meal to last a week."

Amos laughed, holding his hand over his mouth so he didn't show her his food.

"Is that all? Just a week?"

"Well, what can I say? You're a much better choice than all the middle-aged men who hit on me, and tell me they love me."

"The price of fame," he said putting the peel on the table and leaning in to look her in the eyes.

"Who is he?" she asked with a grin.

"Oh, just a writer."

"Just a writer, huh. Even Dawson City has internet."

"No, not Dawson. Just Peggy's and the larger motels. Do you want me to leave?"

"No. He didn't complain or anything. Let's keep it that way, okay?"

"No, problem," said Amos, looking down at the table as he said it.

Sissy got up and started to leave when she turned around.

"Then again, it looks like he's no longer my concern."

She stepped to the side away from blocking his view behind her.

Amos looked up, and his heart stopped. The door to the inner hallway was propped open and Ellison was at the desk with his saddlebag on the floor below him checking out. Amos slid out of the wood chair and stood up. Ellison saw him. Then he did something unexpected. He produced the yellow envelope from the bag, and walked over to Amos.

"It's very good, and you have an amazing talent, but I have nothing to give."

The envelope was just a foot from Amos, but he didn't want to take it back. It was if the words and ideas were solemnized in Ellison's possession. He reached out and took it, his face became flushed, and tears welled up in his eyes. Amos' reaction was unmistakable, and Ellison became embarrassed. He took a step toward him and whispered.

"Look. I have to go."

"If I did something..."

"No. It's not you. I need to find a bookstore. Unless you have a copy of 'The Sea Wolf' there's nothing more for me here."

Amos' energy spiked, and he became a different person suddenly.

"I have a copy. Wait here," he exclaimed pushing the envelope back into Ellison's hands.

"You're kidding." Ellison smiled as he looked back at Sandy who watched from the hallway inside the hotel.

Amos had bolted from the pub, totally unaware of the scene he caused among the two other patrons. They looked over at Ellison and Sissy.

"I'll just have some coffee, and be staying three more nights," he said to Sandy taking several steps toward a seat at the bar.

By the time Ellison had his second cup, Amos reappeared out of breath, and his eyes scanned the room. He walked coolly toward the bar holding up the book.

Ellison took the hard bound copy like a weight had been lifted off his shoulders, smiling.

"Thank you so much," said Ellison. He turned the book to the side, and looked at the stamp on the edge opposite the spine which read 'Cedar City Library.' He smiled wider.

Utah.

Amos caught his breath as Ellison flipped through the pages trying to find his place in the story with the different font and size. Amos backed away, and then turned.

"I'll talk to you later?" said Ellison, closing the book.

Amos nodded.

"You been up the mountain, yet?" he asked.

"Just to Crocus Bluff and the cemetery," said Amos turning sideways.

"How 'bout 8:30 tomorrow morning?"

"Okay," said Amos bashfully.

Behind Amos' youthful bravado, and the forefront of his boundless energy, was a hidden secret and vulnerability. Sissy met him at the double door taking him by the arm as he held it open.

She leaned in, her words delivered softly on his ear.

"Sandy said three drinks are on the house."

Amos half smiled, half looked away. The last thing on his mind was benefiting from Ellison's layover in some monetary way.

Chapter Twelve
The Grand Design

"I sprang excitedly to my feet.
'I wonder, I wonder,' I repeated, pacing up and down.
Maud's eyes were shining with anticipation as they followed me. She had such faith in me! And the thought of it was so much power added. I remembered Michelet's 'To man, woman is as the earth was to her legendary son; he has but to fall down and kiss her breast and he is strong again.' For the first time I knew the wonderful truth of his words. Why, I was living them. Maud was all this to me, an unfailing source of strength and courage. I had but to look at her, or think of her, and be strong again.
'It can be done, it can be done,' I was thinking and asserting aloud." (The Sea Wolf page 315)

The end of the book was as perfect as the setting under a tree next to the Dawson City Museum.

"Finishing a good book is like remembering a perfectly completed lifetime in hindsight, like waking from one of those dreams just as the sun rose on a spring or autumn day," thought Ellison as he watched another group of senior citizens appear from Harper St.

He stared at the title on the cover of the closed book with total contentment. He traveled far in the past few hours. He was neither rushed, nor drawn into the present, but now so grateful for the fact that it was in Dawson he was able to finish this masterful work. He set the book on the grass, picking up the small notebook to his right, and took a pen in hand as he looked over at the book again.

He spent hours afterward in this state of perfect euphoria, writing lyrics and thoughts dictated from the universe, and translated from brain to hand, shifting the position of his legs from time to time, moving to one the benches on the massive wood walkway to the museum. The people who passed ceased to be a distraction as in days past, and he felt part of society, if for the short time he maintained this "zone." As he landed from this state of elation and ecstasy, he looked from handwritten page to book again, and was overcome by emotions. He used to feel like this during the writing process at home with his family around him.

Just on the other side of a closed door, he knew the two women in his life would be there to greet him, and pick up on that ever so subtle peace and contentment he brought out of the room with him.

Then he recognized that this peace was not an act of betrayal for the first time in months. Was he beginning to heal?

Ellison took the ferry across the river, and wished there were somewhere to walked along the river looking back at Dawson. Visiting the Dawson City River Hostel was out of the question, but the view there was impeccable. It was peak travel time back across, but his presence was minute compared to the people who were driving through and tourists aboard. He leaned against the rail, admiring the small, steady waves the heavy ferry made in the water. It was all rather surreal. He imagined the ferry tipping over, causing havoc to all aboard like in "The Sea Wolf."

Imagining 1896, what a different state the small town would be in; buildings teetering into one another as a result of perma frost, susceptible to several major fires which took out whole blocks, not to mention the overcrowded, dirty environment and disease. And Bombay Peggy's would not be on Princess Street. He glanced at his watch and was surprised that it was almost 7 pm.

Ellison went directly to his room, and went through the pub over to The Drunken Goat for dinner. There must have been a break in the delivery of busloads of tourists on the Holland America "assembly line," as he thought of it. It was emptier for the hour. He thought it refreshing to find flowers placed at the entrance table, and at the far side of the bar.

The waitress confirmed the reason for the lull in business. More were expected the next day. Amos walked through the door as Ellison finished his dinner, and he was surprised to see him.

"I'm just here to eat. Not stalking you."

"Sit," said Ellison.

"You sure?"

"Yeah."

Amos suddenly appeared to be an inch taller. The vulnerability from that morning was gone. He was immortal again, "for a limited time," and his expression meeting his lifelong hero face to face again was obvious, but restrained. His walk was confident, and he ordered a coke and an order of French fries. They were at the end of the bar nearest the door.

"Have you heard the news today?" he said to Ellison. "I mean really. Why don't these Republicans just get on TV and say, 'Mr. President. We don't care about the people losing their homes & jobs, only the pretext that you're trying to take our money, and give it to people we don't give a shit about. Oh, and Robin Hood was communist to that kingly regime.'"

Ellison was slightly impressed at this introduction, and looked at Amos with intrigue.

"Where did you get your news from here?"

"Yahoo at the Cyber Cafe on Front St."

"You're a utopian... I gather from your writings."

Amos smiled, and nodded.

"Not everything I write."

"You should start your own independent party."

"Theodore Roosevelt couldn't win as an independent having been president. What chance does any Joe Schmo have. How was your day?"

This question wasn't a boast, but genuine interest.

"It was excellent, actually. In part thanks to you."

"How did you lose your copy?"

"To the river."

"Really." Amos couldn't help but smile. "Ironic."

"S'okay. If it didn't happen to me, I'd think it was funny... It made today's read more powerful."

"Did you finish?"

"Yes. I was almost done."

"Good. Then we can talk about it?" Amos almost hopped in his seat with delight.

"You read it, then?"

"Oh, sure. I finished before I even got to Whitehorse."

Amos' food was delivered, and he went for the ketchup immediately.

"So what did you think?" asked Amos as he hungrily stuffed a fry in his mouth.

"Different than I imagined it would be. I knew that London was a political activist, but I forgot that because of the notoriety of his more popular writings."

"Call of the Wild & White Fang?" Amos blurted out as he glanced up from his plate.

"Yeah."

Ellison stopped for a second to admire Amos for his youth and energy while distracted by his food.

"Don't they feed you around here?"

Amos stopped and collected himself, taking a napkin to his lips.

"Sorry. So, what surprised you most?" said Amos.

"The dramatic turn of events that put Wolf Larsen and Humphrey in a one on one struggle. That and seeing London show his romantic side. It caught me off guard."

"Me, too. And I was so impressed how expert London knew the trade of seamanship."

"That was masterful, wasn't it?" admitted Ellison.

He looked at Amos, and the fondness he felt was frightening. Then a twinge of betrayal resurfaced suddenly.

"Your fries are getting cold."

Amos took a fry as if on command, looking at his plate.

"Guess we wouldn't make very good critics of Jack London," said Amos before stuffing food into his mouth.

"That's because we're not contemporary. It's hard to criticize people of the past, especially a defined classic, when we can be unmerciful to those living."

"Ah. The cynic I've grown to love surfaces."

This comment by Amos drew Ellison into the past. Not because the comment wasn't inaccurate. He looked at him again, but without familiarity as before. Amos was a stranger, a fan who thinks he knew everything about him from a song lyric, or an interview.

"So. What of Wolf Larsen? What made him the character he was?" asked Ellison with renewed scrutiny.

"He chose a life of brutality because that's what life taught him. Even though he envied Hump, and secretly longed to be an intellectual, he knew that in the real world his brutality would dominate others. His nickname for Humphrey was like any bully who calls someone names because secretly he's afraid of him."

Amos finished his last fry, and wiped his mouth for the last time before he continued.

"But he had compassion for Humphrey, and still resorted to brutality toward him, like his crew. It was necessary to maintain his superiority, but had he been compassionate, his ship wouldn't have been scuttled."

Amos didn't know that Ellison was looking for a fight, and continued.

"That's what London wanted. He's an expert at showing opposites exist even in the wild. That's why he injects a woman into the story, to show how man's nature can become stagnant without the perception of women," Amos said.

Ellison found the conversation turning against his own emotions.

"It's the female aspect implied in the word 'mankind' that demonstrates the ability to love," continued Amos.

Ellison looked down at the counter, unable to look at him any longer.

"The most difficult thing for humanity to find," Amos continued, "is balance exemplified in Buddhism. And it's the female aspect of mankind that is unafraid to believe in God."

"Plenty of men believe in God without the aid of women," said Ellison.

"But even the Judaic/Christian religions, which imply the greatest depth of spirituality because of its claim to have direct contact with God, don't teach the concept of 'balance' the way Buddhism does. It's the perversion of religion to either exclude women because she was commanded to procreate, or deem them a distraction from spiritual growth."

"I'm sorry. What does religion and God have to do with 'The Sea-Wolf?' Morality and religion are not synonymous. That's the fallacy among religionists. I think you lived in Utah too long."

"I agree with you. It's sad that some people need to be taught morality, when it should be inherent. But you have to admit that it is easier for women to have faith in faith, than men?"

Ellison didn't answer. By agreeing, Amos diffused a potential argument. But Ellison had enough of the conversation, and Amos for one day. Amos' fault was to continue despite Ellison's docile body language, an immaturity of youth.

"So do we suspend our faith in what we cannot see, and leave the rest up to a wife to rescue us from what you admit may be truth?" said Amos.

"You assume too much. I don't want to talk about this anymore."

Ellison got up, and began to walk away.

"I thought we were just having a philosophical discussion. I'm sorry," said Amos standing up, the rest of the pub behind him.

Ellison tried to smile, but it came out wrong.

I can't give you what you want. I don't know you, and need to keep it that way.

The smirk on Ellison's face was misread by Amos.

"Artists may be anchored in the realism of the world, but we do exactly the same thing Wolf Larsen did. Pull ourselves out of the chaos and into an existence of our own choice. Without us, the world spins into chaos, because inspiration is the source of our strength. You and I are alike."

Amos' comment was like a plea. Ellison sighed and rubbed his eyes, then turned completely facing Amos.

"You're a cool kid."

Ellison wanted more than anything to sever Amos from him, admired that geekiness he shared with him, but was still too polite to just blow him off. He looked into his eyes to see the sincerity.

"G'night."

"See you in the morning?"

Ellison forgot about the invite to hike, and looked at him again. The compassion in his eyes was unavoidable, and he answered involuntarily.

"Yeah. See you then."

Ellison went directly to bed, emotionally exhausted.

There was an obvious awkwardness between them as they made their way up the road in the morning. Amos had seen what he should have in hindsight, after Ellison excused himself the night before, and was withdrawn himself now. He had to break the ice though, be the first to talk. They made a left on Eight St., and down to King which turned into Mary McLeod Rd. He spoke as they began climbing up the hill.

"Have you been to London's cabin?"

"Yeah."

"Amazing, huh?"

"Yes," answered Ellison with as little verbiage as necessary.

They approached the two cemeteries before Amos tried again.

"So sad how young London was when he died. You know, I've had this recurring fantasy since I've been here."

Ellison was silent.

"I've imagined traveling back in time to Henderson Creek, and handing him a bottle of vitamin C. 'Now don't share these with anyone, and if you get the inclination to use someone's ax to break through the ice, don't."

Ellison chuckled to himself shaking his head at the same time.

"That would have been good advice," now thinking about the situation. "We are very lucky."

"Yes we definitely are," Amos agreed. "What a miracle science is."

"And the scientific school of thought."

"Amen."

They made a hard left at a dirt road past the Hillside Cemetery.

"Ever heard of Carl Sagan's Cosmos?" said Ellison out of curiosity.

"Yes. I took Physics 127, astronomy, my first semester in college, and my professor referred to it, so I rented a few episodes."

"Not just Mr. Movie, huh?" Ellison joked.

"No. That first semester was the best. After that, the required courses were just too much for me. I also had Philosophy that term."

"Do you read a lot of fiction?"

"I like classic literature, but lately I can't get enough political philosophy and Carl Jung. You?"

"Usually, I read a lot of that stuff, but... I don't know. Fiction is the only thing that keeps my focus right now."

"Can you imagine being just one thing, or not to be? Have you seen the movie 'Mobsters & Mormons?' The whole movie, all they do is talk about the LDS Church in the 3rd person. Don't get me wrong. I'm not like those anti-people whose sole purpose is to point the finger. All those people see is the demon haunted world. Below average people are like that, psychologically."

"Do you consider yourself above average?"

"Well, you tell me? I flunked out of college. But I'm interested in everything, which is why I try to put myself in everyone's shoes. Everyone's a hypocrite in some way. The day you say to yourself there's nothing I need to change, about myself, is the day you really become one. Even people who stand for nothing, who believe nothing. If you can't sit down and read a book or listen to a speaker, or look something up on Wikipedia for heaven's sake, you're wasting your brain. For what? Football? The latest season of "Bones" on DVD? Ever watched Bones?"

"Couple times."

"I love Bones. There's some really good psychology in there. 'Wrong -ology. Get your grubby -anthro hands off my -psych.'" Amos laughs. "That's from an episode. Sweets and Bones always get into it. Great dynamic."

"You are Mr. Hollywood."

Amos made an audible pause like a "hmmm" in the back of his throat, but it was more of a groan. It was a reflection noise, more feminine than masculine. It made Ellison flashback to a movie he liked, "The Thirteenth Floor," because of the Outer Limits feel it had, where Gretchen Mol made a similar sound.

"No. I just moved out of there after 4 years."

"Los Angeles?"

"Yeah. That's not all I am. I swear. Rahmana Maharshi said there's no way anyone can sit down and describe themselves. Even if you tried, we are each of us so grand, we are indescribable. Or was that H.R. Poonja. I forget."

"You seem well read."

"I'm only 26. What the hell do I know? Joseph Campbell said that we're engaged in life 'til 45 with ideas that give life meaning. After that, we're disengaged. But I don't think everyone follows the same model. Jung would probably disagree too. But Campbell was using Dante's writings as a point of reference."

Now Ellison was impressed by the mention of Campbell. He used Campbell's imagery in his lyrics on occasion, on a very objective scale. He considered Amos as a plagiarist, having studied his own words in music, but his ideas were coherently linked from reference to reference.

"Why do you think everyone doesn't follow the same model?" asked Ellison.

"Well. We all have different experiences, talents, and age, beyond mortality. Age is relative. 'He's an old spirit,' you may say about one person. I'm a young spirit. I say this because I know myself. But some people are born with wisdom. Some are old spirits, but grow very slow. Some incarnate over and over, and some only once because as new spirits they're teachable, like a child. But to think someone's a human in one lifetime, and a cow the next, is not logical."

"Science, the Kabbalah, even the Old Testament all teach that everything starts small, then grows in stature, line upon line. You can't take the intelligence of a man and put it into the size of a bug. In this respect, there is no such thing as reincarnation. It's more accurately eternal progression," continued Amos.

"Dude. You're all over the place," said Ellison shaking his head in disbelief.

Amos stared off into the wide expanse of what was one of the most spectacular views of Dawson, like in a trance, his eyes watered up and tears poured down each cheek. Ellison looked at him in amazement, somehow acquiring an insight into why this emotional response became so apparent. He put his hand on his shoulder. This affection surprised himself.

"Come on. Let's start back."

They doubled back downhill; the small clouds along the east horizon were like on fire. Amos was looking away from Ellison as if he wasn't there.

"You know," started Ellison, "I understand why it's important to try to find something that makes sense of this world, especially when the shit hits the fan."

He looked at Amos, but didn't see any sign as if he heard him.

"The fact of the matter is, we're different than animals because we're self-aware and consciously engaged in a way that is sentient. But we're as unable to control our environment, no matter how much we try. Life is a vicious circle."

Amos glanced toward Ellison, and then at the path ahead.

After a couple minutes of silence, Amos spoke.

"You know that poem by T.S. Elliot about arriving where we started and knowing the place for the first time?"

"Who doesn't," said Ellison in affirmation.

"It has always made me think of a circle. You start at any point in life on this circle and as you make your way around, come to that point where you know yourself, for the first time. And perhaps that one truth, that defining moment is what it all means to exist. In this respect, we create ourselves by our choices. Not physically, but mentally. So it made me think now," he paused, "that all this rhetoric, religious dogma, experience is so we learn to feel what we otherwise would be unable. After all, what is a religious experience? An emotion. That moment where we are touched, feel an overwhelming flood of love, uncharacteristic of an animal, connected to consciousness. Like that line from "A Stranger Among Us," so exquisite it tastes like honey. But if the shit didn't hit the fan, so to speak, if life were perfect, harmonious and without turmoil, it would all be wasted on us."

"I follow you," said Ellison. "But still, there's no proof any of it is real."

"What's real? Everything's an illusion to a Buddhist. You and I know differently. If I hit you over the head with a 2 x 4, the result isn't an illusion. It isn't in our head. But we take the physical world for granted as much as we do the emotions we feel. In fact, we take everything about ourselves for granted. This view of Dawson, our 5 senses. Harrison Ford takes "the force" for granted because he looks the way he does. He doesn't need anything he can't get otherwise. Yet, he didn't create himself, cellular mitosis included."

"Uh, I get your point," sniggering at Amos' choice of an example.

"Getting back to T. S Eliot, perhaps the feelings we can experience are connected to intrinsic truths that give value to the laws of the cosmos, maybe even power. Everything we process is intangible, by our brains. The brain doesn't know the difference. A talent can be used for good or evil. And only that philosophically trained brain actually thinks his or her way through life knowing the difference. Republicans who define themselves as a true devout person wouldn't refrain from compassion. When they say you don't deserve government aid because you're not as thrifty as another, who's whole circumstance is totally different, they're really saying 'I don't love you,' for whatever ulterior motive, usually greed. And to be fair I must pick on my own party. When the Democrat doesn't see the value of such insensitive behaviors, like fucking everything that moves, and lacks the ability to see that personal freedom isn't the I Ching of the universe, they lack the compassion that humanity requires to truly define itself as something more than just another animal."

"Wow, I follow you. I think that Socrates would want to define your use of certain words, and break it down."

"You agree that universal themes or archetypes perpetuate meanings that solicit and inspire altruistic behavior, without hypocrisy?"

Ellison thought over this statement.

"The latter 'without hypocrisy' is essential."

"And the desire to reform or change oneself is individually beneficial, beyond the complexities of that whole Ayn Rand thing?"

Ellison sniggered again.

"I put more value in Plato than Rand, so yes."

"Okay. Now here's the leap." Amos collected himself.

"Of faith?" stated Ellison.

Amos ignored the question, focusing on the train of thought.

"Regardless of whether the ego approves or not with the psychology behind rules of conduct, or even the possibility that the end game is to our advantage, overcoming the natural man and his inclination to do evil is a positive thing."

"Wow. Where are you going with this?"

"You didn't answer the question."

"You're saying that we are children and need rules."

"Yes."

"Then, I'd have to say, yes. But religion muddies the water approaching the absurd."

"Have you read Dan Brown's The Lost Symbol?"

"No, I haven't."

"But you liked the train of thought in London's Sea Wolf?"

"Yes, but I think the common reader has de-evolved because of the way the publishing world and media have underestimated our abilities."

"Could you put that another way?" asked Amos.

Ellison thought a second.

"Because of the way we're fed information in the fast-paced modern world, we're losing the ability or desire to think methodically and form logical hypothesis, generally speaking. Dan Brown may be a perfect example because of the sensational way he entertains his readers. Albeit, there's a genius behind the search for the truth in his stories."

"I agree," said Amos. "You're proving the point I'd like to make. And perhaps it's the fast-paced, modern world that's the enemy of the mind, or shallowness of it. But there's a discussion in Lost Symbol in Langdon's classroom where the student's wish to cut to the chase, and ask him to explain points about the Masonic order without having the proper background, or without earning the right to the answers. Like the original Karate Kid who belabors through all the exercises and perceives being used, but finds that the lessons were in the discovery rather than the answers."

"Laziness." Ellison nods his head.

"Well, when it comes to the deepest, most important lessons, it takes study and discipline to evolve. Mirroring the material world, whether we create ourselves and refine who we become is depended on us. The most simplistic of religious fervor are superficial, but essential. The path is straight and narrow. Now," Amos took a breath and looked at Ellison, "God, being in the midst of spirits and glory, saw proper to institute laws whereby the weaker intelligence could advance like himself. And this is my point. It doesn't matter whether the universe existed for millions of years because the lesson is in the contemplation, not the answer. It doesn't matter whether the Garden of Eden happened, or whether a metaphor. What does matter is what we think... about ourselves, and one another, and yes, that all pretentious 'G' word."

"You're saying that devotion to God isn't paramount?"

"No. I'm saying it is, but the way we perceive it is what makes us develop faith or not. We exist in a world of opposites, where the freewill of another effects us. The most grievous of crimes, to ourselves, is to allow what another perceives as their truth to get in the way of what we do."

"Then why say the world began six thousand years ago?" replied Ellison.

"Because you can't teach the big picture on an infinite scale to a finite people in a pre-industrial/prescience society. Which is why science 'thinks' it has killed God, because they are just as finite today, even with a temporal understanding of the cosmos, but not recognizing that the order alongside the chaos confirms that higher intelligence exists. But we're still influenced by peer pressure. What is so-and-so going to think of me if I'm labeled uncool? It's the perpetual high school mentality. Let everyone worry about their own psychology. We owe it to ourselves."

"So truth is relative, just as age, from your point of view."

Amos nodded.

"It's about change, spiritually so we can change psychologically. If we are afraid of change, then we are denying ourselves. Power isn't in obtaining but in seeking. That's why the selfish rich have to have more. They just don't get it. Whether the imbalance of emotion and reason, emotion and reason," Amos repeated," translates into the whole Borg 'collective consciousness' concept like some religions, where our individualism is extinguished, or the end of consciousness entirely by atheism, both lack balance. What is the reason for consciousness? Life is a huge paradox, full of opposites and contradictions. Do you know that song by Duran Duran, 'who do you love when you come undone?' When life is good, we forget how good we have it."

"That's hitting the nail on the head."

Ellison was plunged into deep thought where anxiety had plagued him the past months, but something replaced it now with a feeling of peace and silence. Maybe it was all this over-thinking. They returned to town and went their separate ways. But he realized that Amos had exceeded his expectations.

Ellison spent the rest of the day playing tourist, took the guided tour from the Visitors Center where doors around town were unlocked to various buildings, going behind the scenes, toured the SS Keno, and played a part as a "judge" in the Palace Grand Theater where real life figures in the history of Dawson participated in a fictitious debate by tour guides.

Chapter Thirteen
Discovery

The next morning was crisp and brilliant; chillier than before. The colors of the trees contrasted the sky and river, post card perfect. It was a sign that summer would soon pass into the dominant winter cold. Ellison had dressed appropriately for his bike. He admitted to himself that it had been long enough since his wheels vibrated over the road. He looked about the empty block, put his helmet on, and then straddled the machine a day earlier than planned.

He would miss Dawson for some time. Its character was imprinted in his brain like the blot of the sun in your eye. He thought of Amos, leaving him behind like Ted and Dave in Bremerton. It wasn't the right time for new friends. But he admitted that something was different.

He'll get over it.

As he roared off, he felt lighter, and the memory of what he lost not as sharp. In a second it seemed, he was on the ferry, dismounted, and looking back at the town. Dawson was a friend that had no more secrets.

Driving off the ferry there was a rush of adrenalin as if he were Clint Eastwood as a retired cop on the run in a 1970's movie, and whose help was suddenly needed in a place he'd never been before.

He tore up the hill on the other side of the river behind the Hostel, and was beyond the view of Dawson for good, not before glancing over his shoulder for that one last look. The cycle was the only morning traffic on the ferry, and the road was all his.

Next stop, Alaska.

It was a miraculous 60 mile drive to the border, but he had no expectations of what the road and terrain would be like. There's a reason it's called the Top of the World Highway, not only to do with being so far north. Most of the Canadian side was paved, but when it wasn't asphalt, it was well maintained this time of year. There were no guard rails, no facilities. Obscure took on a whole new meaning as Ellison slowed down with the turns for safety, chances of unexpected rocks or gravel, and more instinctively, to witness a sight he'd never seen. From the Top of the World Highway, it was like seeing the whole world in every direction, and at a point the mountains were so round and free of trees that he saw a small herd of antelope.

He was happy to feel that exhilaration of an inspection entering the U.S. again. The border agent was typically formal. He looked back at the line of the road when given the "ok," and noticed another motorcycle trailing behind. It was too small to be specific, but must have come from Dawson, too.

He must have been on the next ferry.

Ellison looked back occasionally to see if it was gaining on him. It hadn't, which made him wonder. Quite suddenly, he discovered the difference in the state of the dirt road on the 45 mile stretch until pavement on the U.S. side. It became very rough at points, and he slowed down considerably. The terrain changed as strikingly, too. It became windier, with steep cliffs, and dangerously loose gravel.

Below him was a river paralleling the road. He heard the echo of the motorcycle trailing him as he turned with the mountain. Then suddenly, he slowed down to avoid running too close to a huge black SUV that had pulled completely up to the steep hillside opposite the canyon below. A bleach blonde woman was helping a little blond haired girl of 2-ish pull her pants up after answering the call of nature. The road descended slightly as it straightened, then curved again, the roar of the bike behind growing louder, over the sound of his own. If he didn't know it were there, he might have thought it his own echo.

I didn't notice another cycle in Dawson. Another tourist?...

His thoughts came to another conclusion.

What did she say? Under the table...

He hadn't asked him what he drove, but Ellison spoke aloud into his helmet.

"Amos."

How would he know?

"Sissy," he verbalized.

"They were tight," he thought again.

Just a few minutes more along the road, the motorcycle trailing him aggressively peaked from the curve of the mountain highway in Ellison's side view mirror. But it didn't come along side as he thought it might if it were Amos. It passed him at an unsafe speed. He watched as it did, and was unable to really see who it was. A moment passed and it was around the curve in front of him.

The road was strongest in the middle, the canyon edge possibly suffering from the effect of perma frost. He was warned to drive in the middle, as did other vehicles like buses and tour vans. This would be a frightening place to wreck, and who knew how long it would take emergency services to arrive.

Just when the curiosity of the mystery rider began to fade from his mind, he turned the corner to see him again. Hitting the brakes gradually, Ellison approached the motorcycle who was laid down on its side 50 feet away. Ellison flipped up the visor on his helmet in a flicking motion, and squinted his eyes as he came up behind and stopped. Only the top of his head was visible, the biker's red helmet had rolled a few feet away on the road. He parked his own bike in the middle of the road, and leaped off.

"Are you okay?"

The biker pulled his arm up over his face and head, and Ellison walked around the bike facing the direction they had come. He stood waiting for the arm to drop, and it was now apparent the injured man was intentionally hiding his face.

"Hello?"

He measured the dimensions of the man, glancing over the skeletal frame wrapped around the bike. His leg was pinned, and there were no obvious injuries.

Maybe a broken leg.

"Sorry," said the biker finally. Then, he removed his arm.

"Amos."

"Sorry for the scare."

"Are you crazy?" replied Ellison.

"Depends who you ask."

Amos smiled.

"Let me get your leg free."

Ellison moved to reach down, but Amos stopped him.

"Wait. It's too heavy for you. That SUV we passed. Just wait 'til it catches up."

"Nonsense."

Ellison took a few steps to the side to survey the bike. It was a Harley Davidson. He was surprised Amos had such a nice bike. The custom features weren't cheap, not to mention the engine size. Still, it wasn't so heavy he could lift it a few inches.

"It'll just be a moment or two."

"How's your leg? Is it broken?"

"I don't think so. Scratched up, I'm sure."

"Sure it is. Do you have boots on?"

"Harley boots."

"Well, I must say, you have a nice rig."

"Thanks."

Ellison turned his back on him, walking up-road. He looked over the canyon edge, the forest below showed no effect by man's influence even though this area was littered by the occasion claim. There was a good 100 foot dramatic slope to the river below. Suddenly a black SUV turned the corner and Ellison took several steps in its direction waving his arms. The vehicle came to a stop, as he walked back to Amos' side.

"That's not a good sight," said the dark haired man exiting.

The blonde haired woman on the passenger side was looking out at them.

"No. Not a good idea at all," replied Ellison. "Only someone with shit for brains would be taking these roads that fast.

"Well, what can I do?"

The man had a Russian accent, and looked from Ellison to Amos.

"Well, the two of us should be able to pick it up, if you don't mind?"

"No. It's okay."

The man's accent on "okay" reminded him of the woman in Whitehorse at the restaurant.

They went immediately toward the back of the bike. Ellison put one hand on the side near the seat, the other below the gas tank. As the machine rose off the ground, his right hand moved to the handle bars to straighten them out. He's done this once before, and knew the bike could theoretically fall again if the front wheel wasn't leveled out. To his surprise though, just as Amos was freed, he jumped up like a rabbit as Ellison dropped the kick stand, and ran behind him to the Russian man.

"You! Put your hands behind your head."

Amazed at this sudden outburst, Ellison saw a barrel of a pistol at the man's head.

"What the hell!" he said.

Amos ignored Ellison's comment and grabbed the man by his hair on the crown of his head, and moved him deliberately in front of himself and Ellison facing the SUV.

"What the fuck are you doing, you fuckin' piece of shit," said the man.

The man's pronunciation of 'shit' came out 'sheet.' He started turning to face Amos, but found the metal of the gun drilled into the back of his scalp, and was forced to face the vehicle again. Amos looked back at Ellison at a glance, and moved him and the man two steps to their left so Ellison was directly behind them.

"Amos!" yelled Ellison.

Suddenly, another man jumped out of the back of the SUV pointing a gun at them. Ellison changed his demeanor in the blink of an eye, and followed Amos' lead.

"Now, I don't want to shoot you, and you don't want to be dead," shouted Amos, finding the line from a movie ironic coming out of his own mouth. "All I want is the girl. Take her out, walk her to the other side of the road, and you can all drive off safely! Or!"

"Or, what?" shouted the gunman.

"Or I can shoot you, then your friend here. All that hard earned money will go to waste."

"I don't think my wife wants to give her up!"

The man took a step closer and Amos shot at the ground near his feet. His hostage tried moving to the side, but Amos grabbed him by the hair even tighter, and put the point of the barrel back to his brain.

"You better grow some balls with your wife, now! Do you think she'd be happier in jail?"

"Let me speak to her!"

"No. Just think about it!"

A few seconds went by.

"Talk to him, Mister," Amos said to his hostage. "I swear, if you don't I have no choice but kill you."

A moment passed, and the hostage began speaking Russian to his companion. Another few moments passed and Ellison noticed the gunman kept looking at the vehicle. He tilted his head to the side for better look.

Whatever the two men had said, a decision was made. The gunman disappeared behind the back door that remained open this whole time, and Ellison and Amos heard the woman in the front seat screaming in Russian. Ellison wondered if she would leave its safe confines.

That would complicate everything.

Suddenly, the little girl appeared. She was confused and scared, and began crying. The gunman looked at Amos.

"Over there!" said Amos pointing the gun at the other side of the road. "Leave her there!"

He did so, walking and pointing the gun Amos' direction.

"Ellison. Get behind me while we move." Ellison was impressed at the authority in Amos' voice. Not just in the commands, but in its control. He did as instructed, knowing that Amos was just as concerned about his welfare as the little girl's.

"With the girl with us, we won't be able to follow you. Do you understand?"

"Yes," said the gunman.

He left her alone as she continued to cry, moving back near the door to the vehicle. Amos directed the hostage toward the SUV.

"Get inside!"

Uniformly, as they got closer, the gunman backed into the SUV. Ellison had his hand on Amos' left shoulder as they arced around the vehicle, facing it while reaching the girl.

"Now, have your Mrs. take the wheel. As you drive slowly away, I'll send this man toward the back door. If you try anything, I guarantee, I'll shoot out 2 of your tires. Then you're screwed. Do you understand me?"

"Yes," said the gunman who began shouting at his wife in Russian.

It went down without a hitch. The unnerving part was when the Russian hostage reached the door and disappeared inside. At that point, anything could happen. They could stop suddenly and find 2 gunman turn on them. Even Ellison held his ground before looking at the girl on the hillside. Amos kept his gun honed on the vehicle as it moved farther away, driving around the two motorcycles. At one point, it stopped off in the distance. Amos readied himself mentally for anything. A half a minute later, it took off at a determined speed.

"Probably changed drivers," said Amos as he turned to face Ellison for the first time.

They both stood there a short moment glaring at each other. Amos relaxed his gaze with the gun to the side like he was at Ellison's mercy.

Ellison then simply began shaking his head before speaking.

"What the hell was that all about?"

Freed by the break in silence, Amos went to the little girl, and picked her up like she were his own, patting her back, and speaking to her to quiet her sobs.

"It's okay now. It's okay. You're all right. Do you want to see your daddy?"

"Daddy?" repeated the girl.

"Okay. We're going to take you to see your mommy and daddy now."

Ellison got some of his answers by this exchange, and relaxed a bit. Just then, another car appeared on the bend of the road. It came to a stop near them. Amos explained what had just happened and the couple from British Columbia sat in amazement and disbelief.

"You're kidding," said the man behind the wheel.

The wife got out of the car as Amos took a step back, and handed the little girl to her. She went willingly. Ellison and Amos followed them to Chicken, AK where they reported the incident to the authorities, and were instructed to await an Alaska State Trooper. In the meantime, Amos related the whole story to Ellison, how these bank robbers in Bellingham, WA had shot the father in the leg, and taken the girl hostage. Abandoning the get-a-way car, they had disappeared with close to 2 million dollars.

"Someone's a little self-absorbed. How did you not hear about this?" Amos teased Ellison, whose eyes dropped to the ground. "I'm just kidding. Thank you for following my lead. You thought I was crazy, didn't you?"

"It crossed my mind."

They waited with the little girl and a female desk agent inside the motel, outside at least 10 RVs in the parking lot. Chicken was picturesque, the countryside full of shrubs and small bushes. It was positioned on the 45 mile stretch of dirt road on the American side of the Top of the World Highway. They had passed many short roads leading to RVs, trucks and ATVs along the river where claims were still worked. It was beautiful and obscure.

Up the road from the motel were the Chicken Mercantile Emporium, Liquor Store, Saloon, and Cafe which was the whole of the thriving metropolis. Off on the side of this western storefront, as if out of a John Wayne movie, was a bank of outhouses. Instead of a boardwalk, a very long log served as a break in the dirt where trucks and cars parked up to.

When the trooper arrived, he took Ellison and Amos' driver's license, and stopped short while inspecting Ellison's. He looked up suddenly smiling, and Amos smiled at the man as enthusiastically. The trooper noticed Amos gawking at him, and handed the licenses back.

"Well. Tell me what happened, and how you spotted these bank robbers."

Amos recounted everything, as Ellison nodded at different stages.

"Thanks to you, they've already been apprehended outside Tok. It was foolproof had you not spotted them, literally in the middle of nowhere. Once identified, there was nowhere to hide." The Trooper laughed. "I mean, where ya gonna go? This is Alaska."

"How 'bout the parents?" asked Amos.

"Yeah. About that. They're both on a plane to Fairbanks. Between them and the bank, you gentlemen have a reward coming. $10,000 from the bank and another 5 from the parents."

Ellison was shaking his head 'no' immediately, and Amos just patted the little girl on the back smiling as she slept in the arms of the young woman.

"I'm not accepting anything from the parents."

"Can I ask you a question?" said the Trooper.

Amos looked back and up into his face. He was a monster of a man to Amos' small frame.

"You obviously know how to handle yourself. Why didn't you shoot em? There was little risk, and you were justified."

Amos just nodded his head without replying, and smoothed out the wrinkles on the little girl's shirt. Then he looked back at him, pursing his lips in empathy.

"Let's get going. I've commandeered you with your employer 'til Tok," the Trooper said to the woman.

"Okay," she said agreeing.

"You gentlemen will follow me. I need you to sign a formal statement there. Then I can cut you lose."

Ellison nodded in affirmation. Amos just went with the flow. On the way to their bikes, Amos apologized for detracting him from his plans.

"Like the Trooper said, there's really no other place to go on this stretch of highway."

"Eagle, Alaska."

Ellison smiled. "No."

Eagle was an equally obscure place north where the asphalt began. Ellison straddled his bike, looking around this remarkable place, and lost in a moment's clarity. The harsh sound of Amos' motorcycle kicking to life woke him to action, and he followed Amos' lead again, shaking his head as he wondered how he had got himself into these circumstances. They followed the police cruiser up the dirt road west toward Tok, Alaska.

The lone highway witnessed their arrival like two gods looming from the sky. They roared away like thunder and lightning, and with purpose.

Chapter Fourteen
Rebirth

"I said I listened to it," Shane said to Rowdy as calmly as he could.

Rowdy had bought him a CD to cheer him up, Katy Perry's first album, and was now taking a vested interest in it being played.

"How many times?"

"Probably five," he answered pulling the car into the parking lot of the electronic store.

"And? What did you think of it?"

"Will it stand the test of time like Dream Theater? I doubt it," he said pulling between two white lines, and shifting into 'park.'

"Come on. It's a totally different genre," said Rowdy. "No matter how much time goes by, I can take that album out, and think of the first time I laid eyes on her. You have to admit she's hot."

They left the car and walked toward the store. Part of Rowdy's therapy since Shane and his wife separated was to encourage him to pick out a new theater system since he gave her practically everything. He moved into a studio apartment with nothing more than a twin size bed, and one of the two bedside night stands.

Shane had moved to Medford, Oregon 2 years after Rowdy. It was a complete coincidence that the company he joined after college had moved its headquarters there, Shane being Vice President of Sales & Training. Rowdy owned two restaurants by then, and now expanded into Northern California; one in Sacramento, and another in Vacaville.

"Okay," interjected Shane. "I like it. The second half is better than the first. It's less gimmicky, and her voice gets beyond that whole Alanis Morrisette thing, which is what it first reminded me of."

They were in the store now, heading to the back where neon lights advertised the televisions.

"My favorite song is 'Hot 'N Cold,' because her voice and the melody are perfect together. When she makes a statement about the guy, then says 'no' before the next line, it's like she's answering a question. It's very seductive and well done. Then the second verse builds into the chorus again very powerfully."

"Wow. You have thought about this," Rowdy said taken back.

"It's a curse the way my brain breaks things down."

"Go on," encouraged Rowdy.

"The song 'If You Can Afford Me' was surprising, the way she really puts the importance on love over the material things. I just thought it was going to be another material girl song. And the song 'Lost.' Well, I empathized with."

"Man. Is Ted all wrong. He said you wouldn't like her because of the way you put girls on pedestals. I told him you wouldn't care she used to like black cock."

"Rowdy!"

Shane looked around to see if anyone heard his comment.

"Would you please not be so damn crude? Yes, her music was interesting, and I liked some of it. But that has nothing to do with her personally. What possessed you to buy this particular CD, the cover?"

"Well, that and the fact she was on the cover of 'Cosmopolitan' once. Okay, how 'bout this one?" he said pointing to a 60" flat screen.

"No. It's too big and too expensive. I just want a 19 inch."

"Shane. That's too damn small."

"I don't need anything like that now."

"But you're used to something bigger. If you buy that thing," pointing to a smaller screen, "it'll be a waste of your money."

"I'm going to be too busy to watch much T.V."

"Why? Are you planning on finding God?"

"Rowdy. If this world wasn't such a shitty place, there'd be no need for God?"

Rowdy looked around for other ears like a bad actor in a "B" movie.

"Now who needs to watch what he says? You're going to get lynched."

Shane bent down and picked up a box.

"Really, Shane."

He put his hand on his shoulder when he straightened up, lowering his voice.

"If it's about money, I'll cover you."

"Thanks, Rowdy. But no thank you."

"Hey, you don't have to let her walk all over you."

"What's done is done."

Rowdy followed Shane toward the registers.

Chapter Fifteen
Breathing Room

The highway between Chicken and Tok was like the country racetrack selection of a video game, miles of open scenery with mountains in the background, curved stretches and straight-aways with long horizontal loops up and down that obscure the highway from itself, rivers with wide bridges, and occasional patches of trees along upcroppings of banks where the roads were literally cut into nature. It leveled out into a flat plain in Tok as the convoy roared into the tiny town, a mere outpost in the middle of the forest.

The police station was next to the visitor's center. Between them was a tall plywood framework painted with a male and female Alaskan holding a giant thermometer on ice. Visitors could place their faces in each hole to have pictures taken. It took an hour to wait for the report to be typed up and signed. Amos and the young women had explained to the little girl her mother and father was flying in on an airplane, "all the way from home." She seemed to understand. No one asked Amos to produce his gun, just asked its purpose. He explained that it was for protection from wildlife. Carrying a firearm wasn't illegal in Alaska for this reason.

"You know, I think I'll just stay the here night," Ellison said without looking at him. "The day's shot now."

He looked at his watch.

"I think if I leave, I'll just be distracted and hit a moose or something."

Amos could tell he was edgy.

"Wanna have lunch?"

"I'll grab something after I find a room."

The Trooper walked up, and had them each sign the report. He gave Amos a faxed printout from a Bank with a Seattle address on the letterhead.

"Just give 'em a call. Thanks for your help."

"Where's the girl?" asked Amos.

"She left a few minutes ago for Fairbanks."

Amos didn't ask about the particulars. He was distracted by Ellison's behavior. The Trooper ushered them to the front door.

Ellison went his own way to the Caribou Cabins and checked in. He threw his saddlebags on the floor in frustration.

"Shit."

He was a frustrated with himself, and the fact he brushed Amos off the way he did. For the first time this necessity to push people away seemed genuinely self-defeating and selfish.

"Damn," he exclaimed as he left the room, slamming the door behind him.

Ellison looked everywhere for Amos, but only found his motorcycle parked next to another motel. It finally dawned on him how the Road King Harley Davidson motorcycle didn't fit either Amos' age, or his apparent lack of funds. He tired quickly after going office to office to see if he'd checked in there.

"No, but there was a young man who asked where he could pitch a tent," a man said at the 3rd motel.

"Where'd you send him?"

"Over in the tree line," he said pointing behind the highway.

Ellison exited looking across the street.

"No way."

A few moments later, he made his way into the dense forest, totally isolated and void of fences of wire, wood, or anything else. Then he saw the colors of orange and white ahead. Amos was assembling the tent between the trees. It wasn't even a clearing, and one side of the tent was right up against the tree nearest Ellison as he approached.

"What are you doing?"

Amos turned around wide eyed.

"You scared the shit out of me," he said holding his heart. "I thought you were the police or something."

"Police? Yeah, I'm sure you need to be afraid of police after saving that girl's life."

"We're back in the States now. You never know," he responded.

"Come on. Pull all that up."

Amos did as instructed not questioning why. Ellison watched shaking his head at Amos as he unassembled his tent, leaning against a tree, which literally held him up as he looked down at his feet a moment later at a silver spike that held a corner of the tent taunt. He leaned down and pulled it out himself, his right leg flowing backward like a fulcrum to balance him. It was exhilarating to feel the metal slide out of earth. Several minutes passed and Amos was on his knees folding it up, and squeezing it into the tent bag. When they had made their way to the edge of the woods, Ellison stopped suddenly, and turned on Amos.

"Give me your wallet."

Amos smiled in disbelief.

"What?"

He put out his hand, staring unflinchingly into Amos' eyes.

"Why?"

"Just give it to me."

Amos' hand went instinctively to his back jeans pocket and held it next to his thigh. Ellison leaned toward it, and Amos handed it over. He watched Ellison rifle through the very private, fake leather after stopping first to see the picture of him with his mother, father, and sister. He pulled out the cash, and counted $129, then found the license, library card, old student ID, and an ATM card for America First Credit Union.

"How much do you have on here?"

Amos shrugged.

"Anything?"

"Twelve dollars."

"Which you can't even get out of a machine. How do you expect to get back down to the lower States with this, much less drive all over creation?"

"I'm allowed to get a job now that I'm in the U.S. again."

"Hum. You forgot about that reward."

"Yeah," he said smiling.

"But you didn't have that this morning."

"No," Amos agreed.

Ellison took a hard look at him.

"It's admirable, wanting something so bad."

Ellison realized that the young man across from him had more in common with Jack London than he did.

"But it's also stupid."

"I hadn't planned on staying in Dawson so long."

"Well it's not my fault."

"Of course not," replied Amos with a crinkle between his eye brows.

Ellison came to a conclusion in his mind after a moment, and turned toward the two lane highway through Tok.

"Come on. Put your tent away and let's get something to eat. I'm hungry, and I know you probably haven't had a descent meal since those French fries earlier this week."

"Yes, I have," replied Amos instinctively.

"By the way, how much did that internet cafe pay you for helping out?"

"How'd you know about that?"

"Sissy. Twenty bucks, forty?"

"Coffee, bagels, and internet."

Ellison looked back at him as they walked.

"Not surprised," shaking his head.

"Well, it saved me spending some money... and the internet paid off for that little girl."

Ellison said nothing, but knew the value Amos placed on her life.

Ideals above his own life.

They entered a cafe ten minutes later. A crowd began building momentum, and they were seated in a section that had been closed until their arrival.

"What would you gentlemen like to drink?" said the hostess who seated them.

"Do you have any dark beer?"

"Sorry. Just what's on tap."

"I'll have an ice tea, please."

"You, sir?"

"Not sure yet."

She left, and Ellison leaned in.

"You can have the extra bed to sleep in. I don't want to talk about money, see any appreciation on your part, or any reservations about anything. Okay?"

"Okay."

"We can hang together 'til you get this reward. You can pay me back, not that I care. Total it up in your head, but don't ask me if it's right or anything."

"Thank you," Amos responded somberly.

91

"Uh. That's what I'm talking about."

"Sorry."

"Let's just focus on Alaska."

"Okay," Amos agreed, watching his words.

"It's Friday. You'll have to wait 'til Monday now to call the bank. Just let me know what they say, and keep it at that. A hundred and twenty-nine dollars."

Ellison was shaking his head again in disbelief.

"Have you told your family what you're up to?"

Amos was surprised at the question.

"I can't reach them."

Ellison didn't really register the reply, picked up his menu, and began reading. A moment later, his tone changed dramatically.

"Hum. That salmon looks really good. I wonder if they have it shipped up here from Washington State?"

He looked at Amos with a sarcastic smile.

"Did you come up the I-5 Freeway?" Ellison inquired.

"Yes."

"The Peninsula had some amazing seafood. Looking forward to fresh Alaskan fish."

"Los Angeles has some great sushi restaurants."

"Well. This will trump anything the big city has. You were there 4 years?"

"Yes."

"I can't imagine putting up with the congestion."

"If you live close to Hollywood, you don't have much of a commute."

"What did you do for work?"

"Driver."

"And you tried breaking into screenwriting?"

"Tried."

"You're good. What happened?"

"Catch 22. Can't get an agent without publishing. Can't get published without an agent."

"So no one read your stuff?"

"Twice. An actor has a head shot. Reading 110 pages actually requires effort."

"Well, I liked what I read."

"Thanks. So did friends from acting class or other people I met. But when a so-called professional read my work, they'd just shoot it down, or not finish the story."

"Acting class?"

"Yeah. I took a class at Stella Adler, to get the actors' perspective. And I took a screenwriting class at UCLA."

"Hmm."

"It was hard facing the abject poverty and chaos of L.A., little old ladies struggling to get groceries home."

"But you took at lot out of the experience?"

"It's sort of a love, hate relationship."

"You certainly don't talk the way your characters do."

"That's 'its voice.' Movies entertain by advancing conflict with minimal dialogue. Not like a book where the writer doesn't worry about extra verbiage as much. It's about building character."

"Speaking of, I have a question for you."

Neither Ellison nor Amos noticed the length of time that passed before the waitress arrived to take their orders. They both looked up at her now.

"I'm sorry for the wait."

"I'll have the salmon," without missing a beat.

Amos ordered the same, except a coke instead of tea.

"What's your question?" he said.

"That trooper made a good point."

Ellison looked intent.

"Why didn't you just shoot those kidnappers?"

Amos leaned back in his chair and looked around the room behind Ellison at the other customers before forming the words. Ellison added to his question.

"Does it have anything to do with your L.A. experience?"

"Yes, I've felt a bit superior." The comment was an admission.

Amos thought a moment longer.

"Did you ever watch 'Band of Brothers?'"

"Yes. It was excellent," stated Ellison.

"Remember that 'Replacement' soldier, leading up to when they found the concentration camp?"

"Yes."

"Remember how he reacted to the violence? You don't think there was a reason the writers put him there, alongside his fellow

93

Americans who had seen so much they kinda shrugged it off? Until the concentration camp, they thought they'd seen it all."

Ellison noticed Amos skirted around the answer, but knew he was taking the part of the "replacement" soldier.

"But it would have been safer, for you, me, and that little girl?"

Amos responded quickly.

"Unless the wife retaliated, faced with a dead husband, friend, and jail."

Ellison measured the answer in his mind.

"I hadn't thought of that. Hmm."

"Neither did I 'til now."

Ellison nodded his head looking into Amos' face.

"Do you blame me, for taking that chance?"

"No. I don't."

Ellison looked outside the windows past Amos' gaze.

"You didn't invent the situation. You did what you had to do."

The rest of their time passed casually in the cafe before heading to the motel.

Amos had the bed nearest the door. They went back out, which was a relief to Amos, to the Visitor's Center; a beautiful, commercial-style log building. The inside had an open truss roof with a 5 or 6 foot pitch, and decorated log supports throughout.

The building was 'T' shaped and lined with taxidermied animals, skeletal heads with mighty antlers, informative pamphlets, and tables of displays depicting original cabin life. Ellison and Amos split up while absorbing the exhibits which were more museum-like than just informative. Ironically they both met up again at the most amazing taxidermied pair of wolves in a Plexiglas case. One of the wolves had his teeth bared, and wrinkled skin the length of his snout.

"Wow. That's cool," said Amos.

Ellison leaned in to inspect him closer.

"Smaller than I'd expect though."

"They probably have dog sled races around here."

"It's like the headquarters for it, from what I've read. Tok is the center for trading with local tribes, and the CIA for Alaskan intelligence."

"We came the wrong season," replied Amos.

Ellison looked up at him and smiled. They both shook their heads 'no' simultaneously. They went to a couple gift shops, Ellison continuing his search for the right hat, and Amos admired a dream catcher wrapped in the contrasting colors of brown suede and royal blue twine with white feathers and light-brown beads. Ellison saw him replace it, picked it up, and bought it.

"Peace brother," he said as he slapped it to his chest.

Back at the motel, Amos took a well-deserved shower, and soaked in the hot water for several minutes. He thought that life was a collection of small tastes and rare experiences, the wanting of things always greater than actually having, while turning to the routine of washing his hair. Love and friendship were more fleeting than anything sensory. He relished that moment.

Ellison was reading from Chekhov while leaning against the head of his bed when Amos resurfaced.

"Wow. That was refreshing."

The corner of Ellison's mouth rose slightly. Amos looked down at the mattress and fell on it like a cold-cocked stuntman. After a few moments, he pulled his cell phone out and a copy of Jung's "Undiscovered Self" from his bag. The phone made the factory sound upon starting up, and Ellison looked over.

"Anything?"

A moment passed.

"Nope. I miss the internet."

"We'll pick it up again in Fairbanks."

Amos turned over onto his stomach with a pen in hand, and began pouring over his book. Ellison was first to doze off, and get under the covers. Another hour passed before Amos went to the bathroom. When he came out, he quietly took a moment standing above his bed before turning back the covers, and then sat facing the front door. Ellison opened his eyes as Amos wept quietly, and then turned out the light. He imagined his shadow and a lump of energy under the covers of the dark room, the thick drapes blocking the light from outside.

The mountains reminded Ellison of Colorado as they tore down the highway into the heart of Alaska, and towards Fairbanks. However less populated, there were many more two-lane roads instead of freeway overpasses, long country roads disappearing into the trees, and occasional trucks breaking the monotony of isolation. Sporadic traffic the opposite direction passed them like tour buses heading to Dawson, and RVs, cars, even occasional motorcycles. Amos matched Ellison's speed fifteen feet behind him, and slightly to one side of the same lane.

They passed an incredible array of dry and vine-like riverbeds under a bridge which took in a view of the Alaskan expanse in the direction which was likely southwest. The river was remarkable mainly because of its inconsistency, gaps of mud and banks of wet barges, and after climbing the hill on the other side, another indescribable sight of trees as far as the eyes could see below the crest of the highway, intermingled by more rivers.

They reached what was now called the Alaska or Richardson Highway which stretched to Fairbanks. They stopped at Delta Junction, which had an amazing bakery and cafe as part of the grocery store, behind it an incredible river for a backdrop, which was runoff from its mountain source. The top of the building was decorated with a cache, like the one displayed at the Jack London Center in Dawson, with lines of cable from all four directions holding it up against winds and nature. Then the highway came near the Alaska Pipeline, and at the bridge of Big Delta they turned off to watch workers scale the pipe until security, a man in a white utility truck, informed them that they needed to leave. Men in a small outboard boat stood watch on the riverbank in case someone went into the river.

"Alaska's still a man's man place," said Ellison as they took off toward the bridge.

"You have to be tough, or at least determined," replied Amos.

The pipeline itself had its own bridge for support as it scaled the river. They followed the river until replaced by lakes and ponds. Suddenly they both slowed down, then came to a stop. Ellison looked back over his shoulder to see if traffic was coming. They waited as a moose grazing along the road ate the long grass, leisurely crossing the asphalt, then doing the same on the other side before disappearing into the trees.

"Cool," said Amos before checking his shoulder, then replacing his helmet. He was amazed at the length of the animal's legs, supporting all that weight, something he always felt unusual with horses.

The river returned near the highway again before they reached the North Pole, a speck along the highway that showed all the signs of Santa, far from his supposed actual residence. It entailed wood cutouts of reindeer, a giant Santa Claus statue, and German style buildings with red trim on white background. The attraction accentuated the road, and then was gone. A few miles later, they drove over a huge red splotch with at least a 15 foot circumference in the highway, a point of impact where another animal, most likely a moose, was hit.

Fairbanks surrounded the Chena River as it looped through town. There was exhilaration for both Ellison and Amos similar to Whitehorse because of the history and quaintness of town. There was also a greater sense of native Athabaskan culture in Fairbanks, much to the credit of the Cultural Center next to the old town, WWII memorials, visitors center, and museums.

Ellison dropped a bomb on Amos there after they arrived, having been given advice from a helpful lady who sold the tickets to a cultural event that evening. He decided they were both going by train through Denali National Park, stay a night, and then a train down to Anchorage.

"But what about our bikes?" asked Amos.

"I got that covered. I hired a guy to tow them down on Tuesday. The best way to see Alaska is by train, and I thought, what the hell."

Amos was amazed how Ellison had totally forgotten about any alienation he first had upon meeting, and the freedom the power of money liberated them.

"Great. Why not?"

"All we have to do is meet up Monday morning. The train leaves later the same day at 3pm. So we can drive out to Chena Hot Springs tomorrow, get in some hiking... if you want. It's supposed to be gorgeous."

"Sounds incredible," replied Amos. "I'd like to hit the local Starbucks. It's in the Safeway store a couple blocks from the motel."

"We can hit it on the way to the Athebaskan Cultural Dance in an hour. I could use some real coffee."

"Excellent," said Amos.

Chapter Sixteen
Playing Nice

The days were cooler, and with September less than a week away, this vacation season would officially close around the 9th. The sheer volume of tourists waned, especially among the elderly, but the international scene was undaunted by overcast skies as it began raining while hiking behind the Chena hot springs, but only a drizzle. They weren't amazed at how irregular nature was, since both Ellison and Amos had lived in the Rockies, but the vegetation here was like Washington State.

Ellison was born in the Midwest, and schooled in Indiana. And he couldn't imagine living anywhere there weren't four distinct seasons.

Desert was a part of Amos' life, and living on the edge of it and snow was the best of both worlds. The big city was like the cry of a wolf for nature, and the idiocies of so-called civilization, like the notion of a city encompassing the whole planet, preposterous. And he could never subject himself to the eastern states where you couldn't see the forest from the trees.

The rain had graduated to a steady flow by the time they cleared the absolute tiny locker rooms of the springs. The thought occurred to Ellison that it would be inadequate for the regular tourist season. Even now, he was uncomfortable, almost claustrophobic when a group of Japanese tourists swarmed the inner changing room. To his surprise, Amos produced a quarter for the locker, and assured him that he'd take care of closing it. Ellison grabbed his towel quickly, and went through the rear door.

It led to an inside swimming pool and Jacuzzi. The door outside was another twenty feet, and Ellison followed the path with handrails to the springs. What absolute genius was the whole effect, and how it flowed with nature because of the monstrous rocks which formed the walls of the pool, the antithesis to the man-made indoor pool covered with mineral buildup on windows and corners of walls. Amos took it all in, pausing at the rail, as he admired the stream rising above the rocks, and gorgeous green hills as a backdrop. They had admired the steam off the stream and other ponds before and after hiking.

There were also ducks and geese roaming free, a petty zoo, and an ice sculpture museum. Structures like greenhouses, an authentic wood shed and wagon painted evergreen, and picnic areas surrounded the main hot spring. Horseback riding signs reminded patrons to "kiss their horse and tip their guides." Another sign was labeled "ice skating pond."

The nicest picnic tables along the river which ran past the Springs were reserved for RVs and guests for a price. Two light-blue tractor snowplows sat winter-ready.

They became used to the temperature of the water quickly. Ellison and Amos avoided the fountain in the middle of the pool, and debated its purpose. Ellison quizzed Amos on his knowledge of classic philosophers, who admitted he'd forgotten most of what he'd learned in college, but had a refresher course while reading one of his favorite books, "Sophie's World," a fictional novel with the history of philosophy. The discussion segued to the school system, and how many European countries teach philosophy.

Amos had thought it a contradiction and ironic that the tragedy of the lethal shooting which took place in Norway a few years ago was the very country the author of Sophie's World was from.

"Politics without principles are dead" said Amos.

The thought reminded him of a discussion in class about whether philosophers were better equipped to rule a country than any other.

Ellison observed that philosophy in American schools might offset the unchecked aggression in athletic programs, and drew some similarities to London's description of the men on the Ghost.

"What I really don't understand is how adult males who teach in schools, and participate in these programs, emulate their juvenile counterparts so easily, despite the age difference," said Amos. "I mean, I'm exaggerating the true picture..."

"They continue to live through it vicariously, and never outgrow the desire to win, especially since they're paid to. Did you go out for any sports?"

"No. I was a social retard, and avoided conflict like the plague. You?"

"No. I was never coordinated enough."

"Surprising... Wow!" Amos said inadvertently, looking at a gorgeous young woman who just dropped onto the scene. She was wearing a rainbow colored horizontally striped bikini with brownish blonde hair which darkened after resurfacing from the water. As Ellison turned to see what he'd gawked at, Amos turned his back to her. Ellison noticed immediately.

"Social retard, huh?" smiling ear to ear.

"No," he responded slightly defensive.

"Why'd you turn your back, then?"

Ellison looked at the girl then Amos, who ignored the comment.

"Come on. You shouldn't be so self-conscious."

Ellison got in another ironic dig because Amos was only an inch shorter than him.

"You're not that short."

"Just being faithful."

"To whom?" responded Ellison surprised.

"A girl I met in Dawson."

"Really? Who?"

"Her name's actually Sofie. We met a few days before you arrived, but she had to leave. We spent a few days together."

"A fling?"

"No. She starts college at Northwestern this term. I'm supposed to get out there."

"Chicago is another Los Angeles."

"I know."

"What makes you think she'll wait?"

"We connected."

"Hum. Did you and she...?"

Amos turned a little red, despite the cool rain on his face. Ellison drew his own conclusions.

"That's great, but if I might make an observation. You're the type to get his heart ripped out. It wasn't your first time, was it?"

Again Ellison read Amos' body language.

How did he know that?

Amos turned away from him, and unintentionally met the pretty girl eye to eye. She glided through the water like Aphrodite on a hunt to seduce a mortal, with no indication of malice. She smiled and with a Slavic accent said "hello."

"Uh, oh. She's a Siren," teased Ellison.

"I prefer the Akkadian version of Astarte," replied Amos, throwing this statement over his shoulder with a bewildered expression.

"Either way, you're cast as Tantalus, and it doesn't have a happy ending," volleyed Ellison who assumed solid ground.

The girl swam to one of the giant boulders, stood up in the water, rinsed the water out of her hair by raising her arms up, and running them over her head. Ellison caught this moment at a glance and flashed back to that monumental episode of "Charlie's Angels" when Cheryl Ladd captured his young heart on TV, with this same action. It was the most powerful, seductive memory of his young life.

Amos must have registered the same reaction, because he exhaled, facing Ellison rather than confront her.

"Well, if you're done here, I'm certainly ready."

This comment raised the vulnerability in Amos, and his anxiety complimented his elevated heart rate. Without a word he swam away from Ellison to the closest boulder, and raised his arms up onto the cool, smooth surface. Ellison wondered if it were indecision or a reaction to their dialogue. He tried to imagine he wasn't the cause of this new behavior as he looked around the pool and generous vegetation.

Amos pushed his body away a moment of two later, muscled arms extended with his hands still holding onto the rock.

Relax, Amos. Relax.

He had never been in this position before, not to this degree.

Is it because I've had sex?

Physiologically his body knew exactly what it would be like to slide the pretty girl onto him, and this battle between body and mind was what Amos was waging. He looked up into heaven, and begged for help. At this point, he didn't care about making a positive impression with her. He just wanted it to end. Finally...

The restaurant was similar to the visitor's center in Tok though cozy and small. Stuffed animals and white Christmas style lights in the rafters complimented the age of the building and worn look of the logs. Wine glasses hung upside-down from the wood rack around the bar, and Ellison enjoyed the ambiance from the back corner, their table next to the stone corner fireplace. The tables were fashioned from actual tree segments, the finished, glazed over lines and cracks showing the tree's rings, a cut-a-way of its own history.

He and Amos barely made eye contact, and the former spared the latter of further teasing.

"I think I'll try a glass of wine. How 'bout you?"

To his surprise, Amos consented.

"What do you prefer, white or red?"

"Red sounds good."

"Have you ever had wine?"

"No, but it sounds appropriate."

"Well. It depends on what you order."

Amos was focusing on his menu as he spoke.

"Ever been drunk?" wondered Ellison.

"No. I've have a one drink maximum rule since moving to California."

"That's really smart actually," admired Ellison. He was looking at him differently more and more.

"Thank you."

Amos decided there was no need to mention taking a fancy to "fuzzy navels" before introduced to a "Cuba Libra."

Ellison made recommendations for food that went with red wine. They both relaxed and enjoyed their dinners, when the girl from the pool entered with a slightly older woman, who looked too young to be her mother. She kept glancing Amos' way from time to time. Had he not been so self-absorbed, he might have noticed Ellison's natural attraction to the woman with her, who didn't look a day over 35.

Upon leaving, she beamed a smile over her shoulder, and he waived mouthing "bye."

"We had better keep our wits about us in this drizzle," Ellison said as he straddled his bike. "Do you feel any effects of that glass of wine?"

"No. It's gone."

"Good."

They roared off the gravel onto the paved road back toward Fairbanks. An hour later, Amos was shaking the water from his inadequate and thin protection from the elements. The motel was the light at the end of the tunnel, and all he wanted to do was sleep.

To his surprise, Ellison took a taxi to a movie theater, suffered from the summer media blitz of large crowds, and saw a movie that wasn't his first choice. By the time he returned, Amos was sound asleep. The table had turned as Ellison looked on him with sympathetic eyes. They both were in the habit of rising early, either because of the continual light or awakened consciousness. But none of the sounds while readying for bed roused Amos from sleep. Ellison was assured and at peace as he went to dreamland.

Chapter Seventeen
Denali

Do you know who I am?
You see me from the outside in
I remember saying long ago
But you didn't believe me then

No matter what I say these days
You forget about that positive phrase
I'm not like him or her
Heaven forbid I were

I am experience from childhood to now
Our memory forever true
To yourself in difficult times
We walk in unfamiliar shoes

Don't think I'll zag into depths of hypocrisy
While I'm straddling the middle ground
We may not agree on everything
But your friend I'll always be

Ellison and Amos made a run to Wal-Mart first thing in the morning. Ellison insisted Amos get some clothes and a jacket to augment what scarcely kept him dry, despite the fact he laundered them early that morning. He also bought him proper rain gear which he left in his saddlebags.

"Don't worry about food," Ellison said as Amos longingly looked at the hummus and brie in one of the refrigerators in the deli section. "They have a dining car below the passenger compartment."

"You're kidding. Like 'North by Northwest?'"

"No kidding," replied Ellison at Amos' amazement.

He almost expected Amos' enthusiasm to all the "firsts" he was now experiencing. By the time they left the store, the man who Ellison contracted to haul their motorcycles to Anchorage was waiting near the road of the parking lot. He was driving a Ford F-250 with a large white enclosed trailer attached. Amos looked over his shoulder as they walked toward the building to wait for the motel shuttle to pick them up.

"Don't worry. He comes recommended."

"By whom?"

"The local Ford dealership."

"Oh. Okay."

They lounged around the motel lobby, and had an early lunch to fill the time before the train left. Amos had forgotten to ask Ellison about his movie the night before, the recent installment of Marvel Comics to the screen. Amos made the observation that the reason Marvel was kicking DC Comics' butt at the theater wasn't because Marvel was better, but because Hollywood insisted on reinventing the wheel with its DC characters, plus revealing their secret identity to the love interest to try making it more dramatic.

"I'd love to have a crack at it," said Amos.

"Oh, yeah. Which character," knowing he meant writing a screenplay.

"Swamp Thing. I have an idea that would tie an Alan Moore story line into my own."

"Is that how it works?"

"For me, when you have an original idea that makes an existing character fresh. But the business end is afraid to do something original. They just spit out the same shock 'n awe, when it's the story that makes the movie."

"But Swamp Thing?"

"Are you kidding? Have you read the Alan Moore comics? He also wrote "V for Vendetta" and "Watchmen.""

"Seen Vendetta."

"He's a master at exploring humanity, when you get past the gore, homosexuality, and ultra-violence."

"Homophobic, are we?"

"Course not. I lived in L.A. I endured conversations about it okay to lick someone's butt hole, as long as it was clean. I just don't think anything should be shoved down everyone's throat. Everyone should have equal rights, but we all have it easier than anyone in history. I don't understand why one person's freedoms should infringe on another's. And let's face it, males are dogs. Whether I like it or not, I'm no different."

"Trust me, Amos. You are."

"No, I just mean, we're sexually aggressive, hormonally."

"I know what you mean," Ellison laughed.

"Insensitivity comes in all forms."

"In some of your poetry, it sounds like you're sick of people."

"Sometimes I just want a place to hide."

"From whom?"

"From everything."

"You're very opinionated. Who do you remind me of?"

Amos looked at him out of shyness.

"Thanks."

"Oh, I didn't mean me," he said sarcastically.

"I meant thanks for putting me on trial," he retorted with a smile.

They were an hour and half early for the train. The passenger cars were so high off the track even Ellison was impressed. The sides and ceiling were open Plexiglas reinforced with steel, which gave a hundred eighty degree view. The coach was far from full, and they were assigned a seat per aisle. Their car was staffed with a tour guide, and a bartender, and made aware that that particular car was made of last minute bookings. Regular season reservations had at least a one week waiting period.

When Amos returned from the bathroom, which was downstairs, Ellison got his attention from the seat kitty corner from his.

"Yes," he replied.

"You're feeling better today, right?"

"Yeah. Why?" he asked with a smile.

"Ask the tour guide how long before we leave?"

Amos pulled out his cell phone.

"'Bout another 20 minutes."

"Humor me," he replied, and Amos looked at him suspiciously.

"Okay," he said.

Amos zipped up to the front of the car with his usual youth and zeal, and asked his question.

"That's what I thought," he said and turned around on a dime.

Wheeling around his eyes met with the girl from the hot springs, and his face couldn't help but blush. She smiled her usual smile.

"Hi." He paused and shook hands. "I'm Amos."

"Hello. I'm Asya."

"Pleased to meet you. Are you here with...?"

His eyes roamed to the seat across from her where the lady from dinner that night beamed his direction.

"Oh. Is this?... You're too young to be her mom."

"I'm her aunt. Thank you for making the distinction," she replied in perfect English. "You keep running into my niece. It must be fate."

"Well. The pleasure's all mine," he said turning back to Asya.

"Are you on vacation, too?" she asked, her accent only added to her beauty.

"Yes, in a way."

"Are you studying in school?"

"No. I'm done with school. And you?"

"Yes, I'm studying to be teacher."

Amos looked back at Ellison knowing he was too far to focus.

"Well. You'll have to teach me a little Russian."

She was impressed by this comment, and her eyes sparkled more in the afternoon light.

"That would be good," she said.

Amos had given her a sign, and was now on the spot.

"Well. I'll see you."

"See you soon."

It was like they'd made a date, and Amos tried to figure out what he'd inadvertently started. Whenever she was near him, he couldn't think straight.

"Hope I don't lose it again," he thought on the way back to his seat.

There were three other young men sitting between her and Ellison. He considered her motives.

It isn't like I'm the only show in town.

Then something dawned on him.

Her aunt was right. Maybe the coincidence of fate makes someone more familiar.

"So. What's new?" taunted Ellison.

"Oh. You know. Life."

Amos sat in his seat perplexed.

"Did you find out who she's traveling with?"

"Yeah, her aunt. She speaks perfect English."

"Humm."

The train pulled out, and they sat quietly looking at a University on the hill riding out of town. The clouds were big and puffy, the terrain wide open like in a cowboy movie, with long plateaus and level ranges which followed the rivers under expressive skies. The trip would take only 5 hours, and at that time, Amos wondered about Asya.

They were free to wander, virtually anything they wanted to procure a photograph, particularly uninhibited by the scarcity of other tourists. Amos used the camera on his cell phone. Ellison had a separate digital camera, went to the front to get a beer, and was delighted they had the dark brew he had enjoyed in Dawson. Not long after, the aunt and Asya make their way toward the back of the train. Ellison introduced himself.

"My niece and I were wondering if you gentlemen have eaten?" she said to Ellison.

"Not for a while," he exaggerated, and looked over at Amos, who was locked in a trance with her niece.

"Wonderful," she said. "I admit I've taken many trains across Europe, but rarely this relaxed."

This impressed Ellison, as it intended to.

In the deck below, the aunt, whose name was Katya, indicated for Asya to sit at the table behind them. Amos naturally followed. Ellison admired how this lady blended such elegance and grace, maintaining a femininity still soft and sensual. She reminded him of Grace Kelly though she did not look like her.

He took her hand as she sat, and her eyes matched her smile when her lips parted.

"I promised my niece a good time. I hope you don't mind my forwardness."

"I dare say our parts are not that different, albeit circumstances may be."

"Have you been to Alaska before?"

"First time, and you?"

"No. But it's both business and pleasure. I work for a development company out of Belarus, with interests here. We import and export products and training. This trip is a needed layover."

"What are you exporting?"

"Ceramic tile and dishes to begin with. Culturally, there's a big market in Russian styles, especially in Canada."

"Excellent. And the training aspect?"

"We coordinate an exchange of work experience with different cultures, and languages."

"There needs to be better global unity and infrastructure," said Ellison.

"I agree."

"And I assume you have a network in Russia itself?"

"It's still very difficult managing the bureaucracy. Have you been to Russia?"

"A long time ago."

Ellison explained that he'd been on tour in Europe, and had flown to Moscow. He always planned on returning and going to St. Petersburg because of his fondness for Dostoevsky. Katya asked what kind of band he played with. He downplayed his answer, they ordered, and she paid for herself and her niece.

"How is your salmon?" she asked.

He slid his dish toward her to sample. She did so delicately, dipping the corner of her fork daintily into the pink fish.

"Um. Very good."

"Are you staying in Denali?"

"Tonight. We have to leave on the first train to catch our flight out of Anchorage."

"Short trip."

"Leave me your information. I'd hate to let a future dining partner go to waste."

She smiled so lovely at him, he didn't feel at all put out by the subjective nature of the comment. He knew there were differences in the subtleties of cultures, and it was literal. Ellison glanced back at

Amos and Asya. It didn't take but a moment to learn what he wanted to know.

After they returned to their respective seats, Amos looked at Ellison guiltily.

"It's okay. I approve. She's lovely, and genuine."

"So is Sofie."

"Time will tell. Did you get her address?"

"Address, phone, email... Blood type," he said sarcastically.

"Too bad they're leaving so early."

"Yes." Amos was quiet after that.

Not twenty minutes went by before Katya came back to join Ellison as they looked out at the remarkable beauty. She sat across from him with her legs crossed over the other in such a way that he could not forget. She wore a black dress above the knee, and the way her shapely curves moved from side to side as she spoke was mesmerizing. Ellison had enough experience to know Katya knew her effect on men, but she did not prostitute it. It was a matter of fact, as opposed to manipulative. It didn't matter how oppositely dressed they were either. Amos had told him she had never married, according to her niece. This amazed Ellison, and he was curious why. Amos had since joined Asya up in her seat.

"Have you married before?" Katya said.

We must be thinking the same thing.

"I recently suffered a tragedy I care not to talk about. You are a much better topic."

"I understand. It is nice to meet someone who is fresh. Someone totally opposite."

"Don't you miss your countrymen?"

"I've always traveled, first with my parents, then for work. You could say I have gotten used to people who see the world as a whole stage, as it were, rather than my country as an anchor which draws them back. It feels confining to think of settling down in Belarus."

"I hope you don't think me too intrusive, but is that why you haven't found someone to fully occupy your attention?"

"I didn't used to think I needed that. But recently, the thought has crossed my mind. The older a woman gets, the more cynical she can become. I don't want to become my Grammy, who is so finite she is a slave to her own neurotic behavior."

110

They were entering the mountainous area, and Katya moved to his bench seat as they watched out the window, conversation turning to nature. She occasionally bumped into him as the train wobbled on the track. The train turned on itself as they went around corners, and the other cars became visible; a long deep-gray metal tube with a yellow stripe. The car immediately ahead looked like the cockpit of an aircraft facing them.

The tour guide warned them the chances of seeing Mt. McKinley were unlikely due to the cloud layer as they approached. Ellison was completely aware that this was the smart way to travel, not to mention the company he was keeping. There was no way of seeing Alaska better than train. Even air travel would have limitations. The train would move with the countryside and sleek along the rivers so attentively.

Their arrival was foreshadowed as the one highway neared the train track, and the mountains presented the most majestic and regal statures. Both sides of the track were decorated with exquisitely cut lodges nestled among the nooks of the valley, split by the river. Many were closed, and guests were booked into the few remaining open lodges instead of shuttled in every direction. Ellison asked Katya if she and Asya would like to join them on the evening tour into the park to see the grizzly bears. She refused at first out of modesty, but he insisted it would be a tragedy to come all this way, and not see inside the park.

So the two couples entered the lobby of the lodge together as if prearranged. Ellison naturally mirrored Katya's stoic behavior as he took the lead at the desk, and then deferred to her so she could check into their room first. He leaned over and whispered into Amos' ear as she signed the register. Asya smiled up into his Amos' eyes, then took his arm in ownership.

"What did he say to you?" she whispered in his ear, her lips touching the cartilage and her breathe resonating far deeper.

"I'll tell you later," he whispered back, even though the subject would never come up again.

Ellison and Amos didn't have any more words between the lobby, their room, and back. Amos just smiled at him as they waited for the women to return. When they appeared they went into the adjacent gift shop, and all four picked out a Denali sweatshirt. Katya's was dark gray, and Ellison helped her into it after the clerk clipped the tag off. As they reentered the lobby to wait for the shuttle to the bus which enters the park, Amos handed Ellison a Denali National Park hat exactly like the one he'd been looking for.

"Thank you," he said in surprise.

"Don't mention it," said Amos.

"The one time I forget to look," he said as Amos walked away with Asya.

"You must have other things on your mind," said Katya, a twinkle in her eye.

"Oh. It must be the train ride."

He looked around the lobby for the first time with his hand on the middle of her back, and realized that he hadn't noticed anyone else the whole time since they arrived.

Getting as bad as Amos.

He looked for him. They were near a taxidermied pair of wolves, Asya laughing at a joke as Amos took a hat like Ellison's and put it on her head, holding onto the draw strings below her chin. She took one of his hands in hers and led him away from the display.

Ellison's eyes went from them directly into Katya's, who was watching him, watching them. There was a calm in her grin.

"Are you as happy as your friend, Ellison?"

The question echoed in his mind. He smiled.

"Yes," he thought, but didn't answer.

She let the question linger in the ether. She looked at the somberness in his eyes.

"You're sure of yourself. I can see it."

She kissed him on the cheek, and then turned to look out for the shuttle.

"There it is," said Ellison. "Amos!"

Not an hour past before they were all looking out of a school bus painted grayish-green in the most unbelievable scenery, below them bears in their natural environment. Asya hung out the window, her arm behind her holding onto Amos' hand, which had two emotional views to choose from. He thought of Sofie from time to time, but Asya didn't let him forget her long enough to let his conscience be overcome with guilt. Katya looked at Ellison next to her smiling, and all the classy etiquette melted away as her tiny frame was replaced by the grandeur of the world outside. Next to those bears, Beverly Hills and Manhattan money were insignificant.

Katya looked up at McKinley just as Ellison took a picture of her. She looked at him.

"Please email me a copy of that."

"I will."

She pulled herself away from the window, putting her hand on his chest.

"Sorry, if I get lost in the moment," she said with a smile and looked back out the window. "Thank you for this. You were right."

What is it about nature that gives people a desire to fill their lives with meaning?

Prologue

It was just after midnight before they were back at the lodge exhausted. The morning train was leaving at eight, so they said their "goodbyes." Ellison traded his information with Katya, and Amos sat in the plush chairs in the lobby with Asya, intending to walk her to her door. He kissed her once, and she teared up.

"I wanted you to have this. It's in Russian."

Amos looked at the words in stanza form on the paper Asya had written by hand.

"I wrote it. Maybe someday I can do a children's book."

She smiled through her glazed eyes. Then she gave him a hug and a quick peck on the lips, and ran to her room. He sat there alone for some time before drifting off. After nodding to sleep the third time, he went up to the room.

The next morning, both of them were moody, but Ellison prescribed their own therapy.

"I'm going to hike the Three Lakes Trail. Wanna come?"

Amos nodded.

The trail was just the medicine they needed. The view at various turns presented yet another long lake between the two mountain ranges. They were driven by the emptiness in their hearts, conscious that each moment took their ladies further away, and by the fact that if they stopped long to admire the view they would be at the mercy of mosquitoes. At one stage of the trail planks of wood replaced a segment of the path, and Amos made the mistake of stopping to investigate a tree that toppled by the perma frost, and was bit.

The chipmunks seemed used to travelers and held their ground, one showing its disapproval by yelling its head off.

Rather a chipmunk than bear.

They both read over the instructions in the room should they actually come face to face with one. Upon returning, they crossed the train track again, looking south longingly.

All they had were coffee and a muffin for breakfast. They went to the restaurant in the recreation center next to the lodge for lunch. Ellison broke from his salmon routine, and Amos had the steak dinner with a glass of red wine.

"Second glass?" Ellison teased.

"No, thank you," he replied trying to force one side of his mouth into a smile.

"Aren't we a lively pair?"

"Look what she left me."

Amos handed Ellison the poem, the stanzas unmistakable despite the language.

"You think I'll forget her as easily as Sofie?"

"The fact you have to ask is an answer in itself."

Ellison handed the paper back.

"I'm a son of a bitch."

"Don't be so hard on yourself."

"She lives in Belarus. How the hell would I ever see her again? Even if I wanted to, it wouldn't be practical."

Ellison didn't say anything. The thought occurred to him, but he had the means with no sacrifice to himself. The waitress brought their check. They walked back to the room to get their bags for the 3 p.m. train to Anchorage.

Chapter Eighteen
Paradise Lost

Ellison woke unusually late, but due to the strain of the previous day it was expected. He was surprised to find himself alone. He threw the sheets to the side acclimating to the temperature of the room, and thought about the coming day. He thought of touring with the band again, possibly doing another album, and the personal responsibilities that he'd been away from. He stretched out long, enjoying the cool sheets of the bed at room temperature compared to the covers. He looked at the light from the curtains and wondered about the weather.

It was completely quiet, and he thought about the activity downstairs. Would he be alone for breakfast this late? He looked over at the clock on the bed stand. 10:34 already. He was craving scrambled eggs, and a few slices of bacon. He thought of how long it had been since he'd had French press coffee lightly sweetened with brown sugar, and cooled with half and half. He brought his knees up and swung his legs out, followed by his body, his feet into his flip-flops on the floor next to the bed. After doing his business, he went downstairs.

The trees out the windows were green and lush, and the lake showed evidence of the wind as the choppy waves wrestled with gravity. There were several boats on the water and Ellison squinted to make them out. The view was something he could never get used to in two lifetimes, and he was surprised to find no one around as he reached the island counter in the kitchen. The French press only needed hot water, and he grabbed a ceramic mug, as the water boiled. The cellular phone he retrieved from his pocket had no messages, and he wondered where everyone was. He looked outside, but couldn't see the road, so he waited to have his coffee in hand before investigating.

The cedar door to the chalet two-story structure was accented with a cedar wainscot down the hallway leading to the stone-face around the 3-way fireplace and stairs leading up. He walked to one of the sidelights on each side of the oak door, and looked out at the circular driveway. Then he saw the note on the narrow entry table of the hall, below the large mirror. He looked up at his reflection and next to him a painting his wife had picked out many years ago on the opposite wall behind him. He always admired this effect, and the obvious taste she had punctuated their existence.

He scratched his left buttocks through the light pajama material as he read. Ellison smiled as he heard the voices from the specially prepared dinner the night before welcoming him home from Europe, and the end of their current tour. He admired the grace of the handwriting in purple ink on the card stock, the swirl of the smiley face next to the signature, and the anticipation of their return from town in a few hours.

Ellison turned suddenly at the knock on the door from behind. This instance was frozen as his body simply observed without action. The knock permeated his head again free of responsibility and emotion. He smiled inside himself, and longed to stay in the moment as long as he could. He discovered his right hand now bring the mug to his lips, tasted the rich flavor, the lingering cream on his tongue, and the feeling of warmth the liquid brought to his memories since childhood.

The third knock vibrated him to awareness...

Amos entered from the bathroom with a towel around his waist, and made his way to the hotel door quickly. The room service attendant greeted him as Ellison lifted his head off the pillow, turning to his side to adjust the pillow again. Amos brought the cart inside, handing a tip to the middle-aged man who was not granted entrance for privacy sake.

"I must have dozed off again," said Ellison.

Chapter Nineteen
Anchorage

The trip from Denali to Anchorage was far more remarkable than from Fairbanks; the fireweeds and ferns which laced the sides of the track, to majestic mountains, cliffs, rivers and lakes that spoke volumes of description. Had every writer throughout history tried, the compilation of all their work in one volume still couldn't come close. Credit was due to the tour guide this leg of the trip who warned where to spot an eagle's nest in the trees in advance, or a rare bird's nest in the water, and it was for sure his eyes were especially tuned to see moose that popped its head out of the dense foliage.

They had passed this time leisurely and free of superfluous conversation. The only time either of them ventured below to the dining car was for a change of pace and to break up the routine of the 8 hour trip. Ellison nodded when Amos remembered he needed to call about his reward. They had been unable to communicate normally while traveling. Amos hoped that this financial independence wasn't cause for them to part.

Have we become real friends?

Ellison certainly trusted Amos. He was sure to act as a buffer if the situation warranted it. Who knew when a fan would jump from the woodwork? A fan like Amos.

Was it a miracle of circumstance?

It would be easily put to the test in a city as large as Anchorage, the doorway to Alaska. Thus far, they had only dealt with obscure populations together. But Ellison was looking forward to it. Locals joked that the good thing about Anchorage, was it was so close to Alaska.

It was almost midnight Tuesday night when they took a short taxi ride to the Hotel Captain Cook, named after the British explorer James Cook who discovered the inlet where Anchorage sets. The ground floor was a museum-like display and the style of the hotel a rugged elegance in the downtown setting.

After finishing his portion of the room service food the next morning, Amos went out while Ellison readied himself. He returned with Starbucks coffee and hour and a half later, which Ellison was grateful for. They both hated normal brewed coffee if given a choice. He doctored his drink downstairs as they left, and Amos gave Ellison news that the only way to collect his reward was to go into a branch in Washington State, or stay in Anchorage 3 days so the bank could send a representative. They wanted the transaction to be somewhat theatrical.

"Do you want me to stay behind? You can go on to Seward alone?"

Ellison stopped and looked at him on the sidewalk outside the hotel.

"Do you want to stay behind?"

"Not necessarily. Are you tired of me?"

"Actually, I've gotten used to having you along. Why don't we just stop in Washington when we head back down below. The concierge last night told me about this bicycle path that ran the length of Anchorage along the inlet from downtown to Kincaid Park. Moose are known to live there, right in the city."

"I just saw a place down the street where we can rent mountain bikes."

"See. It's perfect. We can pick up our motorcycles tomorrow or Friday and drive to Seward. I want to see the killer whales on this 6 hour cruise along the coast, if any are to be seen."

"Cool."

They continued walking inland toward the Visitors Center, a log cabin with a grass roof in the heart of downtown.

"And there's this seafood place to die for called 'Humpy's.'"

"Like Hump from Sea Wolf?" asked Amos.

"Well, it's from the hump of a fish, but..."

They both laughed at the irony as they continued on. Ellison had put his new Denali hat Amos bought him on outside the door of the hotel. It wasn't 'til they went into a souvenir shop called "Once in a Blue Moose" that he noticed Amos' hat wasn't from Denali, but said "Zion Canyon" embroidered on it. It was a slightly different shade of off-white or khaki than his.

They spent the entire day wandering downtown, visiting the Cook monument above a view of the inlet, the Anchorage Museum

118

and Thomas Planetarium, and passed the local Hilton on the way to the Railroad station where they had arrived. It was a beautiful historic site with an authentic coal engine on display with brightly painted totem poles from the British Columbia tribes. Amos picked up a railroad letter opener in the gift shop, and Ellison a stainless steel flashlight.

Humpy's was quite a scene for both tourists and locals. They arrived around 5:30, and sat out back at one of the outside tables, next to the wood fence. Even Amos tried one of Ellison's dark beers, this time an Oatmeal brew. They talked about their influences in music as they admired the lively group which sat near the mural on the east wall, under one of the tent covers. The bar was on the north side of the patio on the wall of the restaurant.

Amos preferred classic rock 'n roll, which amazed Ellison, who was grateful when he announced he didn't have a rap bone in his body, accept one of the first rap songs ever, Blonde's "Rapture." Amos was a huge fan of Dream Theater, one of the few bands he ever bought without even hearing.

Ellison moderately emphasized his influences from childhood, but didn't elaborate much because his thoughts on the subject were well documented. Amos replied by simply saying that his ear was tuned to the sweet melody of guitar above all, and no matter how old he got, could never develop an appreciation for country music; with one exception, John Denver.

The subject turned to drummers, and Ellison said he thought one of the best drummers ever, was Carl Palmer.

"He is amazing, isn't he?" replied Amos. "I preferred him with Asia."

It was approaching 9 pm, and Amos spotted several men from one of the tables looking over at Ellison.

"Do you want the attention of some admirers?"

"Not really."

"Is there anything else you'd like here?"

"No. We can go," Ellison said as he got up from the table.

They walked back to the hotel barely speaking.

"I can't believe we're in Anchorage. It's nothing like I thought it would be."

Amos didn't reply. He hadn't thought about any expectations, and just smiled and nodded.

"But you know its Alaska. It's so quiet. There's a still in the air."

The next day, they were out early, bicycled to Kincaid Park and back, and saw a moose with her calf just twenty feet from the path at the edge of the bushes. Other cyclists stopped and watched quietly behind them before continuing on. The cliffs from the path were high above both water and marsh-like plains, across the inlet in the distance snow-covered mountains stood like still shadows, ominous reminders of the treacherous winters. They could see downtown as the cliffs curved around on themselves like the train through Denali. Jet airplanes roared over the path a few hundred feet above coming in for landings, at one point. They veered off the main path toward the homes and condos which were as quaint and decorative as any on the coast in California, one beautiful silver and red front facade like you'd imagine out of Fahrenheit 451 or some other futuristic drama.

A large part of the day to day business in Alaska were done by small aircrafts, just like in the series Northern Exposure, and they could see them take off toward the mountains all day. This gave Ellison the idea of moving across town to the Millennium Alaskan Hotel, which had a lake behind it which housed many float planes with slender pontoons which were mounted under the fuselage. It was a more "homey" side of town, close to the airport, but even closer to local restaurants and natural nuances.

The lobby had a huge stuffed Grizzly bear fully upright on his hind legs, which towered over them, and a polar bear reminiscent of The Golden Compass, behind glass. The lobby had segmented rooms off the front desk, wonderful for reading and lounging, relatively ignored by the fewer and fewer guests, around displays of other animals and a huge stone face fireplace. The hotel restaurant was on the back with a view of the lake. They decided to walk to the Harley Davidson store down the street on Spenard Blvd. just to admire the view of the mountains to the east now covered with monstrous clouds, exactly like the way mists of morning fog would hover over a lake, blue sky above the clouds and on each side. Trees obscured homes from one another 'til the street would open up.

Continuing along the boulevard, they came across a Thai Restaurant that had the most authentic, and amazing food. It looked like it had once been a home, but remodeled, and the owners were also the operators. The woman was also very sweet, with her sparse

English, and warm smile. They each had the Thai Ice Tea she recommended.

Ellison decided they'd stay an extra day, and they spent most of the next morning in the lobby reading, took a taxi to what was an equally fantastic India Restaurant where they had an incredible lamb dish, and then to the movie theater just blocks away from Wal-Mart. They checked out early the next morning, took a taxi to the Starbucks on Tudor, and then picked up their motorcycles and headed south to Seward.

Ellison saw his pod of killer whales and scenic view of the coastline that could rarely be matched. They stayed one night before heading back through the pass, through Anchorage, and stayed the night in Palmer. The next day they arrived in Tok, experienced a weird feeling to be back despite the directness of the route, and Amos was glad to have proper rain gear for the journey. The following day they took the southern route along the Alaska State Highway 2, instead of north the way they had come, and drove directly toward Whitehorse, arriving 2 days later.

Chapter Twenty
Real Time

"We have all first time guests today, Mighty MO who grew up in Detroit, and has become the Neil Young of rap with his mix of jazz and country rock with social themes of war & politics," said Bill Maher.

"Love & war, man," replied Mighty MO with a gracious smile on his face. His tightly trimmed African American hair was accentuated by a lone braid that set on his left shoulder with a turquoise bead.

"And what's not fair about that by any means," retorted Maher. "And we have a lovely lady who you may have heard about in the literary world, author Daphne Gillopi. Her newest book "So, You're A Man: Cut It Off," is on the New York Times top 50 list for the year. I personally cringe just at the title itself," Maher smiled at MO. "Ouch."

"The subject matter is quite innocuous, I assure you," Ms. Gillopi said with an embarrassed grin.

"We'll gang up on you later. I promise," Maher said sarcastically, and looked intently at his last guest. A soberness and intensity flashed in his eyes. The guest himself felt the next beat in his chest and tried to look as cool as a cucumber despite his nervousness.

"My last guest is failed screenwriter turned book author. I feel like I've won some unexpected prize having him here today, Mr. Carl Gomolinski. He just published his 2nd book, which has done well considering his altogether idealistic portrayal of characters. The word that comes to mind is 'pretentious.' I wish to start things off by asking why? Why on Earth would you agree to be on my show?"

"Thank you for that gracious introduction, Mr. Maher."

Bill didn't miss a beat, but dove right in.

"Now, let me get this straight. You're a 'Mormon' and a Democrat?"

"By your tone I assume you're going to try to convert me to the dark side?" Gomolinski smiled.

"Well, played. But don't you feel a slight prick in your conscience every Sunday? You do go to church?"

"Yes."

"Well, please explain."

"I believe the two parties consist of half-truths, but the Democratic Party's premise of free will and emphasis on 'we the people,' taking care of our own, and war against the self-imposed elitism of the rich in harmony with God."

"When you say 'half-truth,' you mean that there is something wrong with the Democratic platform?"

"Absolutely."

"And what would that be exactly?"

"More importantly, when I attended a local Democratic Party meeting years ago, I asked the Chairman in open forum what we were going to do to show people we're not immoral. I was congratulated by many people who felt that the implication that we lacked spirituality was untrue. Its chairman eloquently described the premise of what James called 'pure religion,' meaning it's our responsibility to care for the poor, the widows, the fatherless, and being undefiled. This is what Republicans fail to see and do, badly, when they say it isn't government's job, as if there were an alternative for the disenfranchised. But he knew what I meant, as you do, that godlessness replaces being undefiled. That's the half-truth, that ultimate freedom somehow trumps individual freedom."

"You didn't vote for Mitt Romney?"

"No, I did not."

"But you're a bigot when you judge people because they aren't religious."

"You can't assume what people think and feel just because of how others behave. You're being a bigot now, as if I'm no different than people you loathe who are religious."

"Frankly, I don't see the difference."

"You have to judge on individual merit. LDS are required to love one another. If you meet one who doesn't, call him on it. I'm not a Utah 'Mormon.'"

"Bickering over who's right or wrong is as crazy as religion itself." He looked at his other guests.

"You have a right to your opinion, but I'm just trying to find common ground. We as Democrats don't believe the fairy tale of

123

altruism of the rich, generally speaking, because it's psychologically contrary of human nature, like celibacy, but you cannot deny that mankind is limitless in their potential, and limitless in their degradation."

"And blind faith in a messiah you symbolically ingest each week isn't a fairy tale?"

"It's a reminder that as the master psychologist, God wants to teach the attributes that will facilitate growth.

"You came here to convince me that religion is something I can learn from?"

"No. I came here to tear you a new asshole."

Maher's eyes got big and he laughed.

"Really. Why is that, because you love me so much?"

"Because you're so full of shit that the least I could do is give it another outlet."

Everyone at the table laughed from shock, accept Maher.

"You're setting a bad example for my political party, and I think you should either change your party or change yourself." Gomolinski took a sip of water.

"How dare you come onto my show and tell me what to do."

"You don't want me inside your head, Bill. In the words of Alex P. Keaton to his sister Mallory, 'I can see for miles and miles.'"

Maher's eyes were intense.

"Really. Who do you think you are?"

"Who do you think you are to misrepresent religion, tell lies about Jesus and the mythological Horus, and create an air of contention equally as bad as Republicans. I know plenty of agnostic Democrats who respect people for their beliefs."

"And stick my head in the sand while religion controls the ignorant masses?"

"No. Just find balance instead of polarizing issues. By the way, if your ratings dropped, they'd give you the boot," replied Gomolinski.

"You think you can pull that off?"

"If Republicans are camels trying to fit through the eye of the needle, you're the swine before pearls" Gomolinski continued.

"We're going to take a break," Maher announced to the camera.

As soon as the camera went out, Maher stood up, and told Gomolinski to get the hell out.

"Isn't HBO commercial free?"

"Now, before..."

"Before what?" stated Gomolinski.

"Call security."

"You're a contradiction," he replied. "You're the Jew who doesn't believe in Judaism, and the Catholic who doesn't go to church."

"You're out of here."

"Perhaps it's best your kind doesn't have children."

Maher came around the female guest, and hit Gomolinski in the jaw. He went down easily, but got up as quickly, and pointed to the other side. Maher let him have it again. Mighty MO grabbed Maher, and forced him back.

"Thanks, I needed that," said Gomolinski.

He walked off stage; half the audience cheered his departure, and the other half his performance.

Prologue

Ellison hit the button on the remote turning off the television.

"You don't see that every day," said Amos to the television in the motel room.

"He's perfectly within his right to believe what he does, and Maher should have backed off," replied Ellison.

"He intended to provoke Maher, though."

"But he backed him into a corner."

"Wonder what happened before they came back."

Ellison shook his head.

"They'll be talking about this one for days. Ready?" Amos asked.

"Ready," said Ellison under the covers.

Amos turned the light switch off, and fell backwards on his bed.

Chapter Twenty-One
Intermission

"Why do so many men argue for position? Why don't the Voltaire's and Rousseau's of this world come together in a balanced society? Why do we not learn from history and give credit where credit is due instead of trying to convince the other our point of view is right, for everyone? It is if each man in each successive generation wished to take credit for the very language and words used by generations past, because he has suddenly come to the same conclusion. The answer to the question, of course, is empathy. Neither side is able to stand in each other's shoes, or acquire the experience of the other, for they each exhibit truth."

Rowdy put the letter down on the patio table at Starbucks that Shane wrote, and took the last sip of his cappuccino. Two men in their late 20s, who he had had casual conversations with a few times, exited the store and sat at the next table. One of the men was from an Arabic speaking country that slipped Rowdy's mind, and the other had moved there from West Virginia a few months ago. He noted the swagger of the American was more pronounced than usual.

"Hey. How are ya today, Rowdy?"

"Good. How you guys doin'?"

"Not bad. Not bad at all," said the American.

"And what do we owe this enthusiasm to? Steal another look behind the curtain, or get a raise for cutting back on product?"

Nate, the West Virginian, was working for a pest control company. In a recent conversation, he told everyone present the less actual solution he used on the job to "get the customer by," the more he got paid in bonuses. Rowdy thought it unscrupulous, but it wasn't his nature to judge. He took pride in exceeding expectations with customers at his restaurants, but let his managers deal with those areas he would be considered disingenuous about because of his demeanor or personality.

"The answer would be 'yes,' and 'yes.'"

"And by curtain, you mean panties?" asked the worldly Muslim.

Said (pronounced Si-eed) had an aristocratic air about him, and made fun of religiously devout people from his world. He was not crude, but he was far from virtuous. He lit a cigarette, and blew the smoke up into the air.

"Yes. The panty department is a regular Victoria's Secret to some, but not me. I swear, if I had known girls were as easy as my home state before, I would have moved here right out of high school. Is it because we're so close to California, or has the whole world gone easy?"

"Depends who you talk to," replied Rowdy as a matter of fact.

"Man, and they're gorgeous. Keep themselves in shape. Clean."

Rowdy noticed how his mood was now much different from the tone he felt reading Shane's rant. He figured if Shane were there, he would note that man had not changed any more physiologically, than intellectually.

"Whatcha reading?" asked Nate.

"Oh. It's a letter from a college friend. He's just moved away from Medford after a divorce. I miss him."

"That sucks. Why'd he leave here though?"

"Laid off and bad memories. He needed a change, I guess."

"Did he have kids?"

"No. But he just let her take everything he worked for. She got the house, the car, everything."

"He's a Mr. Nice Guy, huh? They get their hearts broken, and never get over it. I hear it from all my friends who are divorced."

"Well. You'd have to know the guy. He is a romantic. She just turned her emotions off like a switch, and left him in the wind."

"So, she's still here?"

"Yeah," admitted Rowdy.

"You know what would make him feel better?"

Rowdy had a sickening feeling start to build in his belly.

"We should hire some whack job to go hang her from her genitals from the highest tree."

Something came over Rowdy. The image of Shane's Ex-wife flashed in his mind, back to a time when they first got married. The image was of a beautiful lady that was now ugly. Rowdy snapped.

"What the fuck did you say?"

He found the guys shirt in his right hand, leaning down into his face like a ravenous wolf.

"What kind of a low-life piece of shit are you?"

Nate's masculine veneer melted like wax, and Rowdy saw the terror in his eyes as his mouth gaped open.

"Who the hell do you think you are? You're no man. If you ever so much as open your ugly, filthy mouth ever again, I swear, I will close it faster than you can say 'eviscerate.' Do you understand me?"

The white trash was nodding before Rowdy finished his sentence. He let go of the t-shirt. The material stood up in a wrinkled ball below his throat. Rowdy stood over him a long moment, gazing through him before looking over at Said, who was completely still. But there was no judgmental look on his face.

Rowdy went inside, and looked around to see if he needed to justify his actions to management. Finding the place free of contention, he exited the front door.

Chapter Twenty-Two
Segue

It is quite possible that he was unconsciously born that day. He stood on a small hill, alone. He was also unaware of how his actions were disturbing those he traveled with, but this was nothing new. He was often too inside himself. It was perceived as rebellion or weirdness, but he was just being himself, fixed on the hills, the naturescape, the brilliant sky, the texture, color, and formations of the rock. They healed his teenage soul, called to him like a discerning voice from the sky, more powerful than a sonic boom.

How could he expect such an opportunity? The desert had been void compared to the ominous mountains of the past. The other boy scouts had followed directions and the prescribed route somewhere below him.

It was like he could see infinity from whatever vantage point he experienced. Thus was his curse and blessing. But his classmates below were obstructed by the plateaus which followed the river like a loyal bodyguard. It was the higher ground that called to him, took precedent over the task defined by badges or rank.

This odd behavior would not confront him; voices spoken behind his back would touch other ears. Reaching the desired target ahead of the others didn't matter. This wasn't the purpose. It was teamwork and conformity. But society cannot appreciate what it cannot understand in the presence of mediocrity; a god is only appreciated by other gods. Just as one would criticize what they don't understand, another exists who writes volumes on it like Aristotle. An Enoch has only to alienate the poor pagans and believers of simple sensibilities. Nothing is translated by man without the power of a higher consciousness.

Eleven years passed to find Amos crossing the border into British Columbia toward the great Northern Territory on his motorcycle the second week in August. He embellished the $500 to the Border Agents who questioned his financial worthiness to enter, lying about a credit card with another $1,000 on it. Another lie was the permanent address back home that used to be his parents' house. Amos had spanned almost the same distance as Ellison on his first day, slept in his tent next to a rest stop along the Oregon Trail in Idaho. However, he took the most direct route to Bellingham, WA and the border, not unlike that Boy Scout hike 11 years ago near Enterprise, UT.

Taking the longer, more scenic roads of the Peninsula, the ferries, and toll bridges would have been more appealing alongside the dense population and traffic of Washington's I5 freeway, but out of the question. He would prefer it to the I 15 freeway that had played a role his whole life, split his hometown in half, and been the lifeline to and from Los Angeles the past 4 years.

This trip meant more to him than the luxury of a motel room. Ironic that up to around a hundred years ago, sleeping in a tent for the night was routine rather than a sign of poverty. Amos' tent was now a matter of survival like the pioneers of old. But in a world where so many have, and the bar has been raised, he couldn't help but be conscious of that fact as the world spun on around him. But he was still too young and happy for this opportunity to see the difference, compared to those embittered by age and loneliness. He was being called to the most magnificent mountains and landscape on Earth by an undefined voice inside demanding artistic authenticity. Not totally unlike Jack London.

If he could hold it all together inside. The product, he hoped, would ensure a future, put his name on a map of literary achievement, and open the doors for all the potential works yet unwritten. In a word, "money," and validation. The center of the "world's" universe.

The rain had failed to cease through the night, lit by the shadows of trees in an extended sunrise or sunset. By the time the sun did rise, he was aware that his feet were wet inside the sleeping bag.

"How?"

He sat up, inspected the ceiling of the tent, and followed it down to the stitched floor/wall. Water under the bag seemed to magically penetrate where his feet were. He got out of it carefully, and set the bag to dryer ground while he dressed for the day. It wasn't 'til he unzipped the entrance and looked outside that he realized just how the water came in. The field he'd chosen the night before was now a swamp with potholes of puddles, and his tent sat right next to one.

At least the rain pushed the mosquitoes back for a change.

The day wore on as he sped past the freshly water-stamped terrain. By 1 o'clock he found a place to stop to dry his jeans and jacket, reading The Sea Wolf while he waited, and changing in the men's room of the Laundromat. He raced on the fading wetness, guiding the motorcycle on one of the dry tracks left by cars in the road, only to be stopped altogether by road construction, and a line of vehicles miles long on a two-lane highway with muddy shoulders. His stomach growled.

He woke late that night forgetting exactly where he was as he answered the call of nature, speedily unzipping the tent, and rushing to a nearby tree with the roll of toilet paper in hand. The relief was quickly countered by the arrival of mosquitoes attacking his bare posterior mercilessly. It would have been humorous as he spanked himself over and over with one hand, killing the creatures as they struck, and the application of paper with the other, had it not been so aggressive and desperate a sight. He dove into the tent again, zipped it shut, and set out a reciprocating attack on the insects that made it past the front gate, so to speak, their stains leaving marks on the polyurethane.

A day later, he arrived in Dawson City in total awe. The journey was worth more than the inconvenience of healing sores hidden beneath clothing. Particularly welcome was the bunk at the River Hostel, and the bath he heated himself, by the wood he chopped himself. That night he sat by the fire visiting with the other travelers, mostly European, laughing and eating peanuts from the shells offered by one of the other guests. He'd forgotten to eat that day entirely.

When morning came, he opened his wallet to count how much money he had left. He had been forced to pay the whole five days at the Hostel at once because it was cheaper than day by day. At least he didn't have to worry about it. With the one hundred he had left, he thought he'd be able to survive long enough to get to Alaska, and get a job, somewhere. He quickly realized this was a fantasy. The food and coffee was so expensive, he spent $20 by noon. The exchange rate made it worse. So Amos did the only thing he could think of. He went business by business looking for work under the table. Frustrated and depressed, it wasn't 'til he reached the Internet Cafe that he caught a break, lying to the owner he once worked at Starbucks, the man agreed to let him fill in every other morning for coffee and bagels. They didn't even have an espresso machine, thankfully, but the German girl he had working there had the personality of a crumb of bread. He must have thought he was lucky to have Amos.

He spent the rest of the day playing tourist, making a beeline to London Square, and visiting everywhere that was free of charge.

The next morning was hectic and more stressful than moving to Los Angeles with his 15 year old pickup truck. He arrived at the cafe on time, but the doors were locked. The German girl thought she had the morning off, and when the owner arrived, the awaiting customers were in foul moods. Many had gone elsewhere, and the owner knew this. So Amos was rushed to get the coffee brewed, rushed making change with a currency he was unfamiliar with, and felt like a pin ball in a pinball machine bouncing from pastry to cash register to coffee pot. By the time the German girl arrived, the owner had calculated how much he had lost in revenue, in his head, and cut Amos' allowance back to 1 cup of coffee, givin' the fact that Amos had lost 5 Canadian dollars by calculating wrong.

"One cup of coffee for 4 hours work?"

By 1 pm he was beside himself as he climbed the hill above the town along the dirt road. He passed the cemeteries for the first time feeling a strong connection to those who found their way beneath ground, and took the path through the trees to the wood-framed lookout above the Klondike and Yukon.

Chapter Twenty-Three
Sofie's World

She managed a great feat. Not only did she escape the grasps of the suitors hand-picked by her parents, who forced her to attend the all-girl college prep school, but she had sacrificed a life of friends for those she neither cared for, nor desired to ever gaze upon again. She resented the new-found wealth of her father, and the unrelenting cries of her mother who insisted she would have a life they never had.

"Mom. If dad is so wealthy, what is it I need to have, that I wouldn't otherwise?"

Her mother hated this logic. But it was all status and class that got shoved on top of her at 14. The week before she left for Dawson City, several of the failed would-be suitors got together to usher her off to her new life and Northwestern University. They had lured her out of the Catholic Church near Worchester, MA by a present offered to her by a sweet 8 year old girl. Inside, was a dark chocolate cap & gown with a parchment wrapped with a gold ribbon.

"Meet Me Outside!" was written in a female hand with a calligraphy pen.

She wandered outside by herself with a warmth in her heart for a secret friend she might have otherwise missed in the years of attendance. Walking up the side steps, however, she found the troop of four spurned boys on bended knee. They didn't even attend that church. They began to sing Night Ranger's "Sister Christian" choir style with their hands outstretched toward her. She turned to leave as the serenade continued, when buckets of red paint were poured over her, and the guilty parties ran away unidentified as she fought to see her way off the last step.

"Why couldn't I have gone to a real school," she thought as she showered and scraped the paint off her body, her father emptying the car of paint stained blankets worn at outside sporting events. Sofie thought how lucky her siblings would be that she was an only child.

Again, she would use cold logic to reinforce her parents' decision to let her take this trip to Dawson.

"Yeah, cause the people you so wanted me to spend my time with, who you wanted to invite to my 18th birthday party, were so much more fun to hang round. I'm sure they wanted to put a can of dog food in that present."

Sofie took a plane to British Columbia, and a Greyhound bus to Whitehorse. She was ecstatic to get into a rental car, by herself, for the 340 mile drive that was left.

"It'll be safer than the mid-west, and I can meet up with Aunt Patty in Seattle on the way back."

Sofie met the Clarks who were from Toronto at a dinner party with her parents. Their daughter had gone up to British Columbia for her graduation present from a different school, and they met up with her in Dawson. They loved it so much they bought a house there.

Of course there was more to the story behind Sofie's world, and the people she was leaving behind. She was not without fault, but the decisions for her life were always countermanded by her parents desire to be who they weren't for the better part of her life. She would have been happier had they paid off their old house in Pennsylvania, and stayed there so she could continue going to school with the friends she had learned to love. Were there "jerks" at the old public school? Of course. Were there girls she could have befriended at her new school? Sure.

Society, in general, knows "happiness" is tailor-made, but the blanket law or the bureaucratic constant does not understand. Nor do the finite people who simply learn to regurgitate facts memorized in books guarantee those people possess the applicable talent in their field of study. Sofie was aware of the social norms. She just didn't know where it would take her.

Chapter Twenty-four
Miracles

By 1 pm Amos was beside himself as he climbed the hill out of town along the dirt road. He passed the cemeteries for the first time feeling a strong connection to those who found their way beneath ground, and took the path through the trees to Crosus Bluff, the wood-framed lookout above the Klondike and Yukon.

Sofie had taken the road south to the dike along the Klondike River, and walked out past the helipad, up the hill behind the baseball diamonds. She was so alive, she felt immortal. Her life was just beginning, and nothing was standing in her way now. She swore to herself, *Never again.*

Since her arrival, she had gone to the Aurora Restaurant and spent $50 on dinner. She didn't mean to. This was decadent to her, but she enjoyed each unique taste of this seafood plate arranged in a way you see on TV at a New York restaurant. The crème brulee was excellent but she couldn't believe it was $10 for such a little cup. Her mom used to buy this brand of pre-made 16 oz. chocolate pudding in the store for $3. She had languished about town, visiting with people she wanted to speak to, and had invited a few local girls over for dinner the night before. She was amazed that so many people lived in Dawson year round. One of the girls was having an identity crisis at 21, as Sofie perceived it, and had a wild, mixed up spirit that was encompassed by art and literature.

No wonder she liked the idea of an all girl get-together.

The other girl was married and they had bought a house recently. Both of them were beautiful young women in their own way, and had so much to add to Sofie's point of view as she lived through their experiences vicariously that evening.

She swatted away a mosquito as she followed the path through the trees, stopping to read displays along the way about the vegetation growing naturally around her. She looked up at the brilliant blue sky that had amassed above her as the morning clouds dissipated into the afternoon warmth. She took her time, building the anticipation to the end of the trail ahead as it made its way to the cliff above where she'd just walked around the town.

She stopped suddenly as she neared the edge of the trees, which gave way to tall grass, then rounded molten rocks, and finally the lookout. She saw the back of his body clearly, as he leaned against the framed rail, his head bowed and arms holding his hands to his face.

Is he?...

Sofie hung there a moment longer, unsure what to do. Amos turned his body to the side, his left arm clearing away the moisture from his face as he fought back the sobs and took a deep breath.

If I move, he'll see me.

It was like she'd walked up on a grizzly bear feeding in the bushes. When she made a final decision to turn around, he did so. They faced each other and froze. Then he put his right hand up, and apologized.

"So sorry. Here!"

Amos walked toward her on the path, and as he got closer, motioned her to pass by. Even despite his flush, red face, Sofie noticed how handsome he was, impressed that he was thinking of her rather than himself. He walked past, and after getting about five feet beyond her, she opened her mouth.

"Are you okay?" she heard herself say.

He stopped and turned sideways.

"Oh, sure. Nothing a little dip in the Yukon won't cure," he said sarcastically.

Is he serious?

"I'm Sofie. What's your name?"

"Amos. Like 'Sophie's World?'" he said in reply.

"I don't know what that is."

"It's okay. It isn't important. I'm sorry I disrupted your hike."

"Don't worry. I would rather spend it with someone," she said imploringly.

This little comment sent tears to Amos' eyes again. He gasped for breath and turned away from her. She felt herself move to take his arm, and turn him around. She reached up and took his face in her hand, and then encompassed his heart, neck, and shoulders with hers in a soft, warm hug.

Her compassion at that moment was the antithesis to the demons from her past, just as she drove the demons from his. She took his face in her hands, wiping the tears away with her thumbs, and gently kissed his lips.

"You're an angel, Sofie," he whispered so quietly, it was almost inaudible.

He stared into her face, and she saw the little boy in him that his mother once did outside the grocery store so many years ago. Then what happened next was unexpected, especially to Sofie. It was so natural, her instincts took over. Sofie found her fingers on the buttons of her blouse, working their way down to the last one near her belly button. She read his face like a book as Amos' mouth opened in astonishment, and his face turning flusher. Then she opened her blouse even more for him, and reached behind her back to unhook her bra.

The strength went out of his legs. Amos dropped to his knees before her, and she took his head into her bosom. His tears bathed her stomach, and he kissed her all over as she guided him to her breasts. It wasn't until a mosquito caused her to say "ouch" that they looked into each other's face again. Amos came to his old self as he lifted her off the ground as his strength returned, and swung her around in a sure and affectionate hug. She became aware of herself too, as he set her down, re-clasped her bra, and buttoned up her blouse.

"Are you okay?" he said as the tides had turned.

She smiled and said "yes."

"Wanna walk?"

"Yes," she said again.

He led her back to the lookout, and she held his hand behind her as she stood looking at the miracle of nature. They spent the rest of the day learning about each other, and Sofie was amazed as Amos told her about his motorcycle trip. She even noticed the resentment his presence made on the face of the unmarried girl from the night before when they met up again. The evening was spent as two couples and this free spirit got together at the home Sofie was using for her vacation, drinking and eating, and hanging out. A deck of cards was produced, and they played gin rummy 'til 11.

Two days later, Amos walked down the hill before the sun rose in the nighttime light for his Internet Cafe rendezvous, leaving a part of his heart with her. Unbeknownst to him, Sofie had left a hundred dollars in his wallet before saying goodbye. This left him with the most emasculating feeling he'd ever felt.

Chapter Twenty-five
Continuum

Ellison was already in a bad mood. The trouble getting his motorcycle to a mechanic in Prince George, British Columbia was difficult enough, and the atmosphere at the local diner proved counterproductive to the feeling that the world was closing in on him. Amos didn't help the matter. Up until that point, he had served as a productive voice when a fan recognized Ellison.

The man in his early forties kept looking to the side around the head of his friend at the next booth. Ellison mumbled to Amos this fact. He finally turned around and looked at the man with a look of disbelief.

"Why do you keep staring at my friend, here?"

"I can't believe I've run into Ellison Watson at a bus stop in British Columbia."

"Who the hell is that? My friend's name is Grant Larson."

"You're not the guitarist from the rock band Blaze of Glory?" the man said to Ellison.

Amos started laughing uncontrollably as he turned to face Ellison again, and mumbled so low no one could hear.

Ellison laughed a short snort, and shook his head.

It's not life or death, Amos.

But it was enough of a ruse to buy them the three minutes before the two men left, but not before they did a double-take as they headed for the door.

Suddenly, the waitress appeared at their table as a roar of motorcycles pulled up and parked, distracting them as they ordered breakfast. They had been up half the night awaiting a truck that carried Ellison and his bike, while Amos followed them the 110 miles. Ellison kept looking at the girl who took their order, and Amos wondered if he knew her somehow.

The young woman was about 20, maybe 21, small in stature, with brown hair shoulder length, and small butterfly earrings in her ears. The most interesting feature was the Lucy t-shirt from the Peanuts she wore with her apron folded in half around her waist.

Amos watched Ellison, as his own head bobbed from the motorcycle gang outside the window to the girl asking him questions about how he wanted his eggs cooked. He nodded to Ellison subtly, expecting an explanation that never came.

The mood of the restaurant changed as this gang of bikers entered, nine in all, wearing black leather, sporting tattoos, and varying in weight and height. One man blurted out that he had to "piss," as if this news was important enough to the whole cafe. Another man shook his head, and patted him on the back as he followed him to the back of the building.

"Do you want to leave?" said Amos to Ellison.

Ellison didn't respond audibly. Just shook his head "no."

"Your order will be up soon," said the waitress as she passed them to empty the dishes from the next table. The new patrons sat at two booths beyond.

"I'll help you gentlemen in just a minute," said the waitress who expertly acknowledged the bikers.

"You can help me in ways you can't imagine," said one of the men as she headed to the back with her arms filled with plates and cups.

Amos read Ellison's uncharacteristic disapproval at this comment. He looked over at the girl in empathy.

She had her back to them and gathered up their order, which came quickly between a lull in customers. Ellison and Amos followed her with their eyes as she moved around the stools and front counter, and slid the plates in front of them. The aroma of eggs and hash browns filled their noses. They thanked her in unison.

Ellison took his fork in hand, and hesitated above his plate, as the girl went to the tables behind Amos' back, whose ears perked their attention to the rest of the room.

"What would you like to drink this morning," she asked.

"Is it too early for brandy?"

"I'm sorry. We don't serve alcohol, sir," she said literally.

"I was joking. Come on..."

The other men at the table ordered coffee, and Ellison finally took a bite of eggs as he mixed the yoke with the hash browns.

"Me, too, but if you add any touches you want personally, I'll drink from your cup."

"What the hell is it about these men?" said Ellison in a low voice. Amos wondered if he spoke about men in general. The girl had gone to the next table, but as she passed the openly flamboyant and loud biker again, he asked her if she was seeing anyone.

"Yes. I have a boyfriend away at college."

"He is crazy to leave a sweet, young thing like you. How 'bout I give you a ride after work?"

Amos' head moved to the cook's area, but found no one in sight.

"No, thank you."

The man reached his arm out, and took hers. She pulled away as if he had leprosy. Ellison's face was flush. Amos must have seen this, because he was on his feet facing the girl.

"Excuse me, Miss. Could you get us some ketchup. I changed my mind."

She obeyed this request happily. Then Amos broke character, and forgot his role entirely.

"You know, Ellison, I understand a few bikers traveling together, but I think that guys like this pig over here, are suppressing something we just don't like talking about," he stated loudly.

"What did you say?"

"That you're working awful hard to prove that you can still function like a man. I wonder why?"

He was to his feet, but the man across from him stood in between him and Amos.

"You wanna step outside, you little shit."

Just then, the man who answered the call of nature exited the bathroom.

"What the hell is going on, Toby?"

"This faggot just called us homosexuals."

"Is this true?" said the returning biker.

"No. Just him," answered Amos. Ellison pulled on Amos' arm to sit down.

Just then, the waitress returned.

"I called the police."

"Fuck, Toby. Did you start this?" said the man to his fellow biker. "Stuart is going to kick your ass out for good."

140

Just then, the leader named Stuart came out, the smile on his face fleeing in moments. Toby, feeling he had to do something, went up to face off with Amos, who was a foot shorter.

"Toby!" exclaimed Stuart. He flew to his side and looked down at Ellison. The recognition showed immediately.

"Cops are coming," said a biker from behind.

Stuart turned and made a circle motion with his finger in the air. There was no discussion. Everyone left the cafe and took their seats on the motorcycles.

"I apologize to everyone," he said as his gaze drifted from the young girl to Amos, then rested on Ellison.

"You. Outside."

The brute left two steps in front of Stuart. Inside they watched a conversation between the two through the window, and the other seven bikes rode away without them as they waited for police.

Ellison was stretched thin, and he rarely spoke the rest of the day. Amos followed the taxi to a motel, feeling he was in trouble. Ellison went to the room and Amos stayed in the lobby with a book. Upon return from dinner 6 o'clock that evening, Ellison was deep inside himself. He entered the lobby, wondered if he would have to mutter to Amos their room number.

"Do you play?"

Ellison saw Amos sitting at a table with a chess game set up. He stopped and considered it, and then sat without a word. They played their 1st game, Ellison trailing behind Amos' assault, but surprised how much he retained from that night he studied in Bremerton, WA. The 2nd game, Amos whipped him much quicker. Ellison forgot to watch his opponent's every move. The 3rd game was a turning point by the chain of events. By game 7, Ellison took Amos' queen which was on the same row after he "checked" his king. It was worth the loss of a bishop, and Ellison won his first game. After that, Amos won fewer games. They played 'til 10pm.

"I'm exhausted," said Ellison.

"Me, too."

"That was fun."

Amos nodded.

"Let's hit the hay."

Amos followed Ellison to the room where they readied for bed without a word between them. Amos sat on the mattress 'til Ellison was ready for the light to go out. Minutes passed in the dark as Amos played the events of the day over again in his mind. He was too tired to stop this from happening. Then the silence was broken.

"She reminded me of my daughter," said Ellison.

Amos said nothing. They had never spoken about anything so personal before.

Chapter Twenty-six
I Remember Now

The reflection in the picture reminded him of more images than one. It was accompanied with the sounds of happiness, warm feelings of stars and primary colors. His son used to cry from the 2nd floor window on his way to work, and latch onto him the moment he entered that evening. There was a ritual, too. Every night, they would go behind the building to throw out the garbage, and linger with the black skies above.

He held him in his arms as they explored the lights from stars and moon, a father totally devout, content, and at peace. His son didn't stiffen himself, chest to chest on their way back upstairs, like he would at nine.

Two years later, in another city a world away, this ritual changed, and included his daughter; the memory of their two heads bobbing about in wonder, peering out the plastic windows covered with mesh, pulled behind his mountain bike. He worked to gain as much speed as possible to their delight. Then he would push them on the swings before night fell, and race home.

His daughter would cry in his arms whenever another man would speak to her, as he joked about staying that way another thirty years.

These memories were torture now. The pain was as tangible as a cut, but invisible deep in his heart. The carriage was now collecting thick dust in a storage unit, and his children growing without him. He no longer sang them to sleep, or bathed them, or comforted their cries. Long ago, they stopped reminiscing about going swimming, camping around the lake, and playing with the laser light in bed with the cat.

Years would not ease the suffering of the man's heart. The separation would drive them into the mother's arms. Like a double-edged knife, her betrayal would be compounded when they took her side about things children should not be involved in. Again, up was down, and down was deeper than anything imaginable.

He gazed at the picture again with his children on his lap, happy. She had chocolate smeared on her face, and father and son wore t-shirts with the two different batman symbols. His face had a huge smile...

He put the picture on his desk next to the check for $105,000, picked up the gun, and shot himself in the heart. A "thud" vibrated in the empty room as his body dropped. The gun hit and slid across the floor out of his hand until it bounced against the wall.

Chapter Twenty-seven
Secrets

The bluish sky had long, faintly visible streaks of clouds above the line of vehicles awaiting entrance into the U.S. Sure it was typical Washington State weather for this time of year, but the sun baring down on Ellison and Amos was a landmark for them after what they'd been through individually. Crossing the border was taking that step back into normality that went with life, responsibility for the past, and everything that needed to be owned up to. Even if they went about the rest of their life as they have the past several weeks, it wouldn't be the same as it had been. It was this one thing they had in common as they inched their way forward. It was this one fact that made them equal at this moment in time. No matter how short-lived that moment would be.

"No matter where I find myself ten or twenty years from now, I will never forget our time together," thought Amos.

"Thank you."

Ellison must have been thinking something similar, because he was nodding his head in affirmation. Amos noted this. As a writer, he observed and noted what others may take for granted.

The closer they got to the front of the line, the tighter Amos felt in his chest.

"Relax, Amos," he told himself. "It'll be okay."

They smiled at the border agent who took their passports. Ellison looked into the man's face, ready for the possibility of being recognized, but the man barely looked at either of them. When he returned, he asked them to pull over to the American side and await other border patrol. They obeyed dutifully. Two men stepped out of the building and flanked Amos and Ellison's bikes, one to the front and another to the rear. Amos' heart missed a beat.

"May I see both of your registrations?"

Amos looked at Ellison as the one in front left, leaving one armed patrol agent behind.

"I wonder if this has to do with that Alaska incident of yours," said Ellison.

"Do you think their computers are that closely linked?"

He looked the man behind him in the face, almost expecting him to answer. But he didn't.

"I guess not," replied Ellison.

A moment later, three U.S. border patrol agents exited the building and approached. Two of them had their hands on the handle of their guns, as the middle one spoke.

"Mr. Watson, how is it you know this man?" he indicated to Amos.

"We met along the way to Alaska. Why?"

The man turned to Amos, and held the registration up.

"Sir. I'm going to have to ask you to get off the motorcycle."

"Why? What's going on?" asked Ellison.

"I'm afraid this vehicle has been reported stolen, and we have to arrest you until this situation is clarified."

"What?" said Ellison looking at Amos.

The color had completely gone out of Amos' face, and tears were welling up in his eyes. He stepped off the bike, and the officers immediately took him by the arms, and placed handcuffs on. Amos looked at Ellison in bewilderment.

"It's my bike," he said in reply to the look of confusion on Ellison's face. "He promised me it was mine."

This left Ellison to wonder even more who "he" was. Did Amos really steal a motorcycle because of some verbal contract?

Two border agents escorted Amos to a police cruiser parked on the line for just this type of situation, one opening the door as the other led him toward the back seat.

"Ellison. Help me! You know me! I'm not a criminal!

Ellison looked back, but then faced his bike again.

"I can't help you, kid," he mumbled to himself.

"You coward! You know me!"

The policeman held him by the cuffs, and guided his head inside.

"Ellison. Gods don't worship other gods. Like them you denigrate yourself out of a false sense of humility!"

The door closed, stifling Amos' voice on the last syllable.

The officer who stood behind Ellison addressed him.

"Sounds like a raving madman who sees things clearer than we like to admit."

"Go easy on him. He found those bank robbers in Alaska who kidnapped a little girl."

"That was him? Don't worry."

When a border patrolman opened the door to the cruiser to get inside, Ellison heard Amos state flatly, his voice docile; defeated.

"I love you!"

The words cut sharp into Ellison's heart. He was surprised at his own reaction; a quake inside his sturdy frame. Numb, he swung his leg over the saddle, and kicked the engine into a healthy roar as the police car drove away ahead of him.

Ellison drove across the border by himself, as he did weeks ago. But what had changed in his heart was unexpected. Ellison really did feel lost, so he thought of the road ahead as he had before. But something else had changed.

He drove on unsure where he was going. He just kept driving. All around him the world was going about its business. Ellison finally wondered what day it was...

Chapter Twenty-eight
Full Circle

The sunrise was magnificent. First the landscape was just shadows. The trees in the foreground were sentinels ominously standing watch over the world as people slept, implants from the golden skies that burned the horizon like gold trim on a present from otherworldly intelligence. Time passed. The mystery in the shadows filled the imagination safeguarding the possibilities in moments lost as soon as concentration was broke. The clouds which hung over the yellow dirt, plateaus above and rocks near and far like a dome eating up the gold stream of light as the ribbon on the package was unwrapped.

Ellison witnessed all of this sitting alone straddling his motorcycle. He watched for some time, afraid to move on from this remarkable moment of peace and tranquility. He didn't want it to pass, but as the light engulfed Billings, Montana, the man-made structures made it impossible to remain connected to nature. He pushed the thought of where Amos was at that exact same moment out of his mind as soon as it surfaced and replaced it with the primal urge for coffee. He had arrived the night before, staying at a motel along the freeway, after taking the direct route through Spokane, WA and Coeur D Alene, ID.

He protected his anonymity, picking the Super 8 in St. Regis, MT the first night back in the U.S., accidentally slept in the next morning, and covered Montana the previous day. Ellison was amazed how wide it was, and just how different the eastern part of the state was to the mountainous west. Happily, one of the local Starbucks was in the bottom floor of the Crown Plaza Hotel downtown, his next destination for however long he'd stay before moving on to Little Bighorn. He had cruised the circumference of Billings to get a bearing on the lay of the land along the way, awaking very early, and stopped to watch the sunrise.

The Crown Plaza was amazing and almost made him wish it were winter. The lobby was nothing short of grand; a huge fireplace on the outside wall opened up to a chalet view of the second floor railing above, and the stone and marble molding accented by the sharp angles of the artwork opposite the fireplace, which reminded you of the geological composition of Billings itself. Starbucks was on one side and the check-in counter on the other with plenty of comfortable couches for seating in front of the fireplace, and around the seating area. The restaurant was on the 20th floor, and kitty-corner across the street from the Starbucks door was Jake's Steakhouse.

Billings was like a big, small town. The desk agent informed him that local shopping was due west, and if he wanted to get a birds-eye view, he could drive up to the airport on the plateau. He grabbed the book "Replay" by Ken Grimwood a fan had sent him from his bag, having finished his Chekhov short stories, and his Denali hat, and headed down to Starbucks. With his dirty Chai latte in hand, he settled on a spot near the docile fireplace under the seclusion of his head gear. He was immediately hooked by the story, and read for some time before noticing the caffeine jitters in his chest.

"Mind watching my spot?" he asked a business man across from him.

The man nodded, and he left the book open to his place.

He returned from Starbucks with a bagel and cream cheese. As he ate, he picked up the book again and read the inscription from the fan inside the cover. He forgot what it said from back in Colorado. His eyes got big, he shook his head, and audibly said, "no shit," setting the book down next to him as he took another bite. It read, "Enjoy, Amos!"

He read half the day before stopping. No wonder Amos had sent it. He could see it made into a movie easily, and it reminded him of "Groundhog Day" with Bill Murray.

Jake's Steakhouse was excellent, and he rushed back upstairs to read. Ellison finished and closed the book around 3 am, and looked at the cover with new-found appreciation. He laid back and stared at the wall opposite him. This went on for minutes, his eyes getting heavier and heavier. Ellison finally got up and turned off the lights, pulling off his clothes and throwing them on the chair next to the small table, falling into bed as if this was the last ounce of strength he possessed.

The next day he slept in, took the desk agent's suggestion, and drove to the airport. There was a small museum where he parked. He drifted from object to object from the past, but not really absorbing their meaning. Billings was below him as he mounted his bike, realizing that the town was in a huge gully. He imagined what would happen if the Yellowstone River escaped its borders, perhaps as a past era millions of years ago. The man inside the museum had just told him that the original settlers thought the place was full of gold deposits because of misinterpretations from local Native Americans. Thus the name "Yellowstone" described the color of the terrain, and void of gold unlike Dawson City.

He drove to the new theater outside town on the flats, saw a movie, and had a yogurt at a shop a few doors down before heading back to the hotel. Ellison admitted he loved Billings, but decided to move on looking out the window from the 20th floor of the Crown over a plate of trout. He felt a sense of exhilaration with the prospect of seeing Little Bighorn, and the wind of the open road.

The elevator opened to the lobby, and Ellison rounded the corners to the Starbucks. Immediately he noticed a man in his twenties sitting alone at one of the tables next to the windows with a chess board all set up to play as he got in line. The man kept looking around and noticed Ellison looking his direction, and nodded. Ellison nodded back and wondered who he was waiting to play as he ordered his Chai latte, minus his usual espresso shot. It was his second one today. Drink in hand, Ellison walked over and forced a smile.

"Who are you waiting to play?"

"Anyone who comes along," replied the man. "Pull up a chair."

Ellison sat across from him as they exchanged names, and began to play. Ellison thought the man wasn't very good immediately, and wondered if he was following his lead. Before long, Ellison took his queen.

"Been playing long?" he asked.

"A few years."

"Hmm."

It wasn't long before Ellison checkmated him, and they began again. He began getting bored while executing his own agenda and the game just seemed wrong. Then the young man did something very suspicious. He had his knight out in a defensive posture, as he should to counter Ellison's knight. But then he sacrificed it for a pawn for nothing. The man just smiled like he had seen something in Ellison's soul he thought funny.

"Why did you do that?"

"What?" he replied.

"You threw away your horse for nothing."

He shrugged.

"Are you letting me win?"

"Why would I do that?"

"I don't know," Ellison admitted accusingly. "I'd rather you played to win. Why are you holding back?"

The man smiled, but there was superficiality in it. Ellison immediately saw something he didn't like in the man.

"Well, thanks," he said getting up.

"No, wait. You don't have to go. I'll play normal."

"You should have played that way from the start."

Still wearing that stupid grin Ellison started to leave.

"Hey, I thought I would take it easy on you, you being a rock 'n roll legend and all."

He had turned back for just a moment totally disgusted, and walked away.

Chapter Twenty-nine
Recession

Shane left the office of the general sales manager of the car dealership like a kid from school after visiting the principle. He entered the private office known as the BDC, Business Development Center, where salesmen made phone calls and followed up. Only one other salesman was there at his desk, his back to him as Shane grabbed a sold customer printout from his desk. The noise made the man turn around, and nod.

Shane pulled out his cellular phone, and thanked a lady for her purchase the previous day. Before he turned to leave the room, replacing the form in his desk, the other salesman spoke.

"Did Burt chew you out for not getting long?"

"Yeah," replied Shane.

"Scott doesn't hate you because of you. He hates you because management hired you."

"That's reassuring. I don't know how to respond to that."

"There's just not enough business to go around. I know you're new here, but you're going to learn it isn't about what the customers think. You can get perfect surveys all day long, but you aren't going to last if you can't get everyone to like you."

"That sounds like a catch 22."

"What does that mean?"

"How can I get along with people if they hate me for simply being here?"

The salesman said nothing, and Shane left the room.

That night, Shane packed up his car. Before closing the door to the empty apartment, he shook his head, and wondered how anyone would ever appreciate him and who he used to be again. He missed his friends.

Shane drove out of town without calling Rowdy in Oregon as he promised.

Chapter Thirty
Into the Light

It was only four days since crossing the border from Canada, and Ellison looked up at the Devil's Tower in northeastern Wyoming with satisfaction sitting on his bike. He remembered how much Amos had wanted to see it since watching "Close Encounters" on DVD. But now here it was. Ellison saw Close Encounters at the theater while still young. It was nothing short of magic, and he imagined night falling and aliens descending from the sky.

What is real, what we imagine, or what we experience?

He admitted to himself that he may not be Mr. Hollywood like Amos, but how so many experiences in his life were from movies and books.

Ellison thought he needed to find another bookstore, and something to occupy his downtime. He dismounted and went into his saddlebags, and held the books he'd finished in his hand. The stamped edge of The Sea Wolf caught his attention.

Cedar City, Utah. Must be from Cedar. He was right next to me, and I never asked him.

His mind traveled to his next intended sight-seeing place, Pine Ridge and the Badlands National Park in South Dakota.

"Wouldn't that be totally cool to do a sweat lodge," he heard Amos say in his mind.

Ellison shook his head.

"Son of a bitch!"

That little shit got to me.

He realized how easy it would be to back track to the 25 freeway and down to the I80 west.

At least I wouldn't have to go through Colorado.

Colorado made him think of what started this whole thing. He started laughing out loud, stepping away from the bike, but then his laugh turned into sobs. He cried for several minutes, and then realized he wanted to be a part of the world again.

I've taken it for granted.

He knew this wasn't true.

I'm ready to take it to a new level.

Then he remembered what Amos said as he was hauled off.

... gods don't worship other gods.

He wondered to what extent that meant. Ellison replaced the books, mounted the motorcycle again, and spun out in the dirt toward the highway.

Chapter Thirty-one
Rock Bottom

He'd had enough. It wasn't just his past life. It was the absurdity of the lack of direction all around him. The thing about being homeless was how Shane appreciated the simplicity of modern technology. He no longer cared about the kind of car he drove, just the fact that he had one. He realized it was better to be homeless than car-less.

"A man without a horse is like a man without legs," he thought, reminded from this line from The Man From Snowy River.

The trick was not letting anyone know. This was easier than he thought. As long as he had somewhere to wash his hair daily, he was fresh, and for all intents and purposes, clean. After all, when you can't cook, you can't eat as much without spending a lot of money. It was funny how little he could survive on. And when you aren't eating you're not... So your extremities and other regions didn't need cleaning as often. He changed into clean clothes daily, and washed them weekly. He lived on coffee in the morning and dinner around 5 or 6 pm. He shaved every other day at a grocery store bathroom that actually had a sink inside with privacy, or at McDonalds. His sleep schedule was more like a farmer than a corporate money-monger, and he took care of business before most of the world even made it out the door.

With the modern invention of the internet & Starbucks, he put together his future on the computer from nothing. It wasn't even tempting to use the money Ted had put into his savings account. As long as it was there, waiting, Shane knew that someone out there was thinking of him. Once the ten thousand dollars was gone, the universe owed him nothing, and that's what he'd have; nothing.

He dropped 15 pounds in one week. And it made him realize just how glutinous his past life was. He'd gone from a college graduate working for a prominent company in charge of an entire sales force which generated millions per year, a house in the suburbs, and a beautiful wife (whom he considered the epitome of love), to almost nothing. Once that love was gone, he had nothing, and now he was richer than the biggest fat-cat in Manhattan or Rock Hill, NH.

Shane Purdue's greatest natural talent was an intuition about the nature of things, especially people, which made him wise beyond his years, or a knowledge in reverse compared to those who both admired and despised him for his rise in the company so young. The irony of it all was, like the song by Billy Joel when he "came home to a woman that I could not recognize, when I pressed her for a reason, she refused to even answer. It was then I felt the stranger kick me right between the eyes."

Chapter Thirty-two
For the Love of God

The town was split in two, the ominous and grandiose mountains on one side and the home covered hills on the other. He wondered just how the residents with homes on the majestic mountainside actually drove to them. When he left the sporadic traffic of the I15 freeway, there was a satisfying feeling in his heart. Such places like this and Billings, MT held high regard to Ellison because they were large enough to be suitable and sustainable without being totally inconvenient to those living there.

"This town has a 4 year university?" he thought after seeing a billboard and the stadium along the highway.

He pulled into the lane which embellished a lighthouse next to the WalMart, and turned right, immediately into the local Starbucks. After changing it up with a vanilla latte, he took the instructions of the girl behind the counter driving down Main St., which literally was the main drag toward the local library. The streets crisscrossing Main were numbered, and as he approached what he was told to look for, a park on the right hand side, he was surprised to see it set up for what looked like a concert.

Ellison made his way to the library parking lot which set on the other side, a grayish brick building facing the mountains. It was early afternoon, and there weren't many people around the stage or booths which lined the borders along the streets of the park. It was obviously in preparation for a community event.

Upon entering, he went to the front desk with the library book in hand.

"I believe this is overdue," he said to a pleasant-faced woman with one large eyebrow.

She scanned the book, and the computer beeped.

"I'd say it is," she said looking up with a larger grin."

"How much?"

"Ten dollars and fifty-three cents, but..."

Her voice trailed off, and then she looked up.

"I'm sorry, but... this can't be you."

"No. The person who checked it out, lent it to me. I just never got around to giving it back. I'm sort of a book fiend. I have a hard time letting go of something when it becomes a part of me."

Ellison wondered why he was explaining himself. Then he attributed it to the authority figure librarians always held in his mind from childhood. Even his high school librarian was a dominant personality. Then again it could have been guilt. Ellison genuinely liked that hardboard copy and entertained keeping it.

"The date of birth gave you way," she replied.

"Oh. Uh... By the way. I was wondering if anyone could tell me if they know where I could find Amos."

"I can't give out addresses," she replied.

"Well, off the record maybe."

Ellison looked around behind the checkout desk at the other workers. The woman followed his line of sight, and initiated the scenario further.

"Amanda, could you come here?"

A girl in her early 20s walked over, and smiled.

"Hi," she said.

"Do you know this person?" asked the first librarian.

Amanda looked at the computer screen, and nodded.

"Yeah. Sure. It's so sad."

The girl's whole countenance changed, and as he looked at her she just shook her head.

"What?" said Ellison.

"His family."

She looked at the much older librarian, then back at Ellison, uncomfortably. She cleared her throat.

"I'd appreciate it, please. He's become a friend."

"Well, I remember him. His sister was a grade ahead of me. She and her mom went traveling abroad, and... they both died in a tsunami. I forget where."

"What?" said Ellison in horror.

"Oh, I remember, just a year ago," said the first woman. "It was terrible. His mother's name was Beverly."

Ellison looked at her.

"And then..."

The girl got really uncomfortable.

"It's okay," said the older woman.

She looked at the computer putting the name with the events.

"That was his father. Oh, my."

She looked up at Ellison again.

"What?"

"His father committed suicide in the back yard. I guess he... couldn't take it."

Ellison was dumbfounded, and couldn't believe what he was hearing. He just shook his head.

"Maybe 5 or 6 months ago."

"Who's motorcycle?" he finally mumbled to himself.

"Pardon?" said the older lady.

"Nothing."

Ellison pulled out the wallet from his back pocket and handed her a twenty.

"You know, we've replaced this book already."

She gave him back his change, and handed him the book.

"I know what you mean about loving a book. I could never love an electronic book."

She smiled at him as he took it. He replied very soberly.

"Thank you."

Ellison was in a daze, thinking back over the time they spent together as he crossed the threshold outside the library. He looked at the mountains above. They seemed more dominant.

He thought about all their conversations, his expounding politics and religion. He thought about how much his writing meant to him. Finally the image of Amos setting up his tent in the forest of Tok, Alaska imprinted in his mind.

The solitude... The absolute loneliness of it.

Ellison wondered if growing up under these mountains would make a person different than someone who didn't.

He became aware of himself when a man approached the library on the sidewalk.

Ellison drove around the town wondering if Amos was there, now. He went to the university and stopped at the statues of history's greatest minds, like Galileo, Shakespeare, and Socrates. The plaque stated it was dedicated by George H.W. Bush.

Sure Amos thought that a slap in the face.

Ellison considered asking two students if they knew him as they approached, but thought it futile. Then he got an idea.

He jumped on his bike and checked into a local motel by Marriot. In the nightstand he pulled out a phone book, and called the Cedar Police Department. He felt stupid as he listened to himself try to explain the situation at first. He finally came up with a lie that might work.

"I have some property of his that I need to return. Surely, somebody knows something. It only happened six days ago. He had Utah plates on the bike."

"Hold on," said a very stern voice.

Ellison wondered if they simply left him on hold. Finally, the same voice returned.

"If I were you, I'd try the Southwest Behavioral Health Center."

A millisecond later, there was a click of the phone hanging up.

Ellison turned to the white pages and found the address. Within minutes, he pulled up to the building and parked. It wasn't even a mile away.

"Hello. My name is Ellison Watson, and I'm looking for someone."

"Just sign in your name and the patient's.

He did so on the clip board in front of him.

"Please have a seat," said the man on duty.

The corridors were empty and the sterile scene was austere.

What do you expect, Ellison?

About ten minutes later, a man appeared from a door down the hall. There was a sign perpendicular to the wall over the door but it was too far, and too small to see.

The man was wearing a white lab coat, and greeted him.

"Mr. Watson?"

"Yes," said Ellison standing up.

"I'm Doctor Parcel. I must say, you're the last person I expected to see here."

"Why?"

The doctor smiled, but not as a fan.

"I mean, Amos has spoken of you at length."

"He's here then?"

"Yes. And I'm glad you came. You are the one person on this whole damn planet that might be able to facilitate his recovery."

"Me?"

"This way."

They entered the door to the office Parcel appeared from. He took off his lab coat, and grabbed his keys from the desk. They went out another door at the rear of the room and through several other doors to a corridor. The doctor slid a little metal sheet open which was a window to a patient's room and stepped aside. Ellison looked through.

There on the bed was Amos, curled up in the fetal position, a pillow between his legs, and a sheet draped around the top leg that rested on the pillow. His upper body was not covered.

The doctor watched Ellison intently, allowing him to take his time. When Ellison took his attention away, he noticed just how deeply the doctor looked at him.

"Why are you looking at me like that? Occupational hazard?"

"Not exactly."

He closed the window.

"Follow me."

They slowly walked back the way they came.

"I look at you as the other half of the coin."

"How so?"

"You and Amos. That's what you are. Two opposites, both true, and both in need."

"Sounds like a bunch of Freudian crap to me."

"Not Freud. Jung."

"Carl Jung? Then it's something Amos would say."

"He did."

The doctor stopped and smiled at Ellison.

"And it proves what Jung believed, that the human brain has the potential to heal itself. But not without self discovery. Amos has replaced his family with someone he never had."

"Jung?"

"You."

This startled Ellison. They returned to his office.

"See. I plan writing a paper on Amos after he leaves."

The doctor opened a file cabinet, and pulled out a huge yellow file.

"I'm in awe how everything I studied for years has crystallized in one patient."

"Aren't you being a little melodramatic, Doc?"

"You tell me. I love this kid. And I can't imagine what person wouldn't. But then again, I'm an educated man."

He pulled something from the file, and dropped it in Ellison's lap.

"Normally, I'd be concerned with privacy, but knowing Amos, I don't need to ask him permission where you are concerned. By the way, he had a really bad day today. I gave him something to sleep."

Ellison looked down at the stack of paper bound together with a brass clasp in each three hole punch. It was a script, with Amos' name on it as the author.

"Can you imagine a father, hating his own son so much, that he would be jealous of any attention his wife gave him?"

"No. I cannot."

"Ah, another educated man."

"No. Just self-taught."

"So that's one thing you and Amos have in common. I don't suppose you know what happened to his family?"

"I just found out. That's why I'm not surprised he's in here?"

"A personal loss and tragedy. That's another thing you both have in common."

"Coincidence."

"Of course," the doctor said to be agreeable.

"Why did his father hate him?"

"I'm not sure. An abnormal inability to show empathy toward your own offspring is most likely a deep seeded hatred learned by one's own father. But since he isn't around I can't ask him."

"And his suicide? What does that tell you?"

"Confirms his father's lack of identity. From what I can gather, it was Amos' own mother who shielded him from his father. He doesn't say it, but... There was an incident once. My guess is..."

"An educated guess?"

He sat on the desk and took a deep breath.

"He wouldn't hurt his son, out of fear of losing his wife and daughter. Hatred of other males is primal. An underdeveloped human who can't know the difference between social norms and hard-wire the brain to accept other males is frightening. Normally, human males will socially bond with other males better than females because they speak the same language. But when his mother and sister died, Amos' father would rather blow his brains out in the back yard, than share the rest of his life with his son, if even vicariously."

"Wow. Is Amos screwed up too? I mean, with everything that's happened?"

"No, he found two ways of replacing his father long before. One, was you?"

"How?"

"Your music, your lyrics, and the guitar. As Amos entered adolescence, he found a rebellious way to define himself with your music, and the band, of course, unlike his father. Much like a boy who never knows his father would."

"That isn't so uncommon."

"Each individual has to come to terms with their own identity, just as a boy raised by a mother often redefines himself through role models outside his family setting."

"And if they don't, they become a mommy's boy."

"Exactly. And he statistically, on the one hand, ends up in divorce because mommy tries controlling her son who has become her surrogate husband. Or he marries someone who treats him like crap; because he doesn't feel he deserves to be loved, on the other hand."

"This is all theoretical, Doc."

"I thought you liked to debate? What has happened to you that you now don't even present yourself as the intellectual giant people expect?"

Ellison shot the doctor a look of pain.

"This is just as much your crisis as his?"

"Getting back to Amos... You said there were two ways he replaced his father?"

"The second was God, or as Amos puts it, the Psychology of God."

"What does that mean?"

"Well religiously, he believes God is literally his Father."

"He's more theoretical than religious. He openly criticizes people..."

Parcel interrupted him.

"Yes, he criticizes people for their hypocrisy, but not religion itself."

"No one should criticize anyone. Amos is no exception."

"Why would you say that?" said the doctor out of pure intrigue.

Ellison felt he had to engage the doctor after his last comment about being an intellectual.

"Hypocrisy has a duplicity that is disingenuous."

"You mean duplicity that a person has to appear one way to his peers, and hide what he really thinks philosophically? Or do you mean losing your virginity at 26, and openly detesting Mitt Romney are not contradictions?"

Ellison looked genuinely uncomfortable.

"By the way, Mr. Watson, don't think you'll offend me."

"Please. Call me Ellison."

"There's a difference between hating someone and expecting them to live up   what they say they believe. In this respect, everyone is a hypocrit   cause everyone is human. But we often don't hold ourselves up   ie same standard we do others."

"Th   a did. Everyone has the right to choose who they are."

"F   nany Thoreau's do you meet these days, or Carl Jung? And wh   i of Amos do you think isn't human?"

    n't judge anyone."

    course you do, or you wouldn't have traveled with him.

    ison nodded his head.

)o you understand the pressure of being a teenager, and not
jur   eving an ideal, but actually living it? You do. But most people
c?   insensitive. These days, you can be an adulterer, Republican
(nor, and be accepted back into Hollywood."

"The ethics of business and politics mirror each other."

"True Lies. But that kid in there hates his own hypocrisy. So
ich so he'll make mistakes, but then correct it. He'll face it head on,
ork through it, and bring himself back to center."

"Read about what to do in a book," Ellison said nodding his head empathetically.

"Empathy is the capacity to recognize emotions that are experienced in other sentient beings, without which we're unable to experience compassion," said Parcel.

"And why we're unable to learn from the mistakes of the past."

"Amos sees the spiritual aspect from the inside, through his innocent perspective, idealizing what he genuinely loves. You don't think spirituality is perceived as pretentious as being drawn to music with such high and lofty themes and philosophies?"

This brought Ellison to see himself, full circle.

"What about this?"

Ellison held up the script.

"Let's talk about that in the morning."

Ellison got up, feeling like he'd been on the couch. The doctor shook his hand.

"Thank you for your time."

"Thank you," said Ellison, wishing he'd been more his old self.

He left, grateful for the fresh, cool mountain air, and stopped in awe. The slope before him was about a seventy degree angle, and he shook his head at the lights of cabins and homes that dotted the giant shadow overtaking the world like an avalanche.

He watched the other patrons from a corner booth at the Chinese buffet, and relished the green beans and broccoli that filled his plate. Ellison felt at home here, more than he did in Colorado, where he had gone to such lengths to avoid people. In Cedar, he was just another person, like in Alaska.

Chapter Thirty-three
Into the Frying Pan

This was the first time he read something written by Amos that was complete and in screenplay format. It was as articulate and grandiose as the mountain outside the window of the motel. He had written a story around the rock 'n roll opera to Queensryche's "Operation Mindcrime" album called "The Hate In My Eyes."

It started out with a montage of the main characters' exploits as FBI agents fighting organized crime to the song "Anarchy-X/Revolution Calling," and how they built both a friendship and reputation leading right into a specific face-off with known mob figures. Ellison shook his head at comments written in the margins from someone who obviously critiqued it. He didn't know the right word was "covered," in Hollywood terms.

Ellison repositioned himself against the headboard with pillows behind him as he got deeper into it, ready for the long-haul, and unable to put it down. At one point, another comment in the margins made him close the script again and read the words Amos hand wrote on the cover.

"Logline: After a mob hit claims his partner and partner's wife, an FBI agent is assigned to hunt a political/corporate assassin, but the closer he gets the more he is convinced his old partner is alive, the very person he is pursuing."

Ellison found his place again and looked at the comment.

"Crazy," he thought.

During the read, Ellison grabbed his phone and downloaded the Queensryche album, and after finishing the story, he laid in the dark listening to it with his ear plugs.

"...and I got shivers down my spine when the line 'the hate in my eyes always gives me away" were sung.' That's where Amos got the title to the story. I mean, I can see this as a major blockbuster summer movie. I don't understand how this person would write what he did."

"Like?" asked Doctor Parcel.

"Like, what was the motivation for Griffen to start killing people?"

"Why do you think Amos wrote a story so violent?"

"Well, it's obvious. Griffen is the wrath of God. What person in America isn't convinced that greed and bureaucracy goes unchecked? Rational people that is. And I suppose you'd say, he was angry subconsciously due to the relationship with his own father."

"So, what does this bureaucracy prevent?"

"Lack of progress and change. Change for the better."

"You weren't offended he used another band's music to tell an underlining story?"

"Course not. The lyrics said what you couldn't say conversationally."

"You think he condones violence?"

Ellison tilted his head. He was fresh today, and saw the reason for the psychologist's questions.

"Come on, Doc. You don't have to be a shrink or Hollywood exec to know that people watch movies like this to let off steam."

"Does it replace doing something about it?"

"For people who feel they have no control over it. Do they amuse themselves to death, like the book with the same title implies, as a way to escape reality? Sure. But why not? Ignorance is bliss, but the opposite is more tormenting, that consciousness brings madness. You have to find a way to balance the two."

"Three," stated Parcel.

"Three, what?" replied Ellison.

"Another thing you and Amos have in common. He is young and you are middle-aged. He is dirt poor, and you are extremely wealthy. He is religious and you are philosophical, but as opposites you've come to the same conclusions about life. As Jung asserted, opposites who appear to contradict one another, can both be right, and come to the same conclusions."

167

Ellison wasn't offended at this analysis. He was, for the first time, proud to have Amos elevated to his level. For the first time he really respected him because of what he created, for what he spent the previous night reading, and everything else.

"How is it you know so much about him, in such a short time? Or did you know him before?"

"I only knew of him because his story was news in this small town. But this facility isn't a permanent treatment center, and as you know, Amos is pretty forthcoming and easy to talk to."

"And what did he say this morning when you told him I was here?"

"I didn't."

"What? Why?"

"Sometimes... you just have to let people blow off steam. I did tell him I had a surprise, and that it would make him happy. So, he's been stewing that over for several hours."

"You are really a master manipulator, Doc."

"I have to be good at something," he said sarcastically.

Ellison stood up.

"Well, let's go."

Amos watched the door open, but couldn't believe his eyes as Ellison walked inside his room. He started crying, and then began apologizing, his hands over each side of his face. You could only see his bright eyes, nose and mouth. What was visible of his face was flushed, and bright red.

"Ellison. I'm so sorry. I didn't know about your family. I wouldn't have been so selfish. I'm so sorry."

Ellison was shocked to see him in this state of panic, uncontrolled. He shook his head, and stood next to him, taking the arm closest to him by the biceps.

"It's okay. It's okay, Amos. Don't worry about it. Shit."

Ellison laughed that this young man was so worried about him. Amos had never seen Ellison really laugh, and it disarmed him. He put his hand behind his back near Amos' shoulder blade.

"What the hell are you doing here, Amos? We gotta get you into some real clothes. This place sucks."

Amos looked down at the hospital pants and gown, as Ellison looked toward the door. The doctor watched on and nodded his head.

"It's not like he's suicidal, right?"

"Hardly," said the doctor.

Ellison looked back at him.

"And what's going on in this town of yours. They've got a stage set up at the park like they know what rock 'n roll is."

"It's the university," said Amos full of hope, beaming at Ellison who wasn't hiding the old persona he once was.

"Well, Doc?"

"You sign a release that you're responsible..."

Ellison looked at Amos. His eyes were like glass with water spilled from a cup of tea. His face was like a five year old boy looking up into the face of a parent.

"Of course. That's what friends do."

He smiled. Amos reached up and hugged him. It took him by surprise, but no matter how uncomfortable it made him feel, his mind pushed it out of his head.

This is normal.

"What are we going to do about transportation?" said Ellison.

"Go pick up your motorcycle."

Doctor Parcel said it factually.

"The man who bought your parent's house resold it the same time you took your dad's bike, which was part of the sale. When he found out who stole it, that you had a set of keys, he said it belonged to you."

Amos and Ellison looked at one another in amazement.

"Come on. I'll get him his clothes so he can change."

Ellison waved as they started to leave, and Amos sat on the edge of the bed. The doctor stopped and whispered in Ellison's ear, just visible from the room.

"I want him to see us conferring. His reaction was healthy. Angry people react aggressively. Makes you wonder about people in jail verses people here."

Ellison nodded as he thought it through.

Chapter Thirty-four
The Chorus

The sun was low in the west, just above the hills of Three Peaks Park with the whistling of the wind and cries of birds for entertainment. The tires of their bikes were covered with dust. A rabbit scurried past them, and it reminded Ellison of Billings. But the desert playground was far from Montana. The vast expanse of flatland produced farms to the east until the majestic range above Cedar. Ellison took it all in as they waited for one of them to speak. He looked at Amos, who seemed at peace for the first time Ellison had known him, nothing to prove and nothing to say.

That's a first.

"It's amazing," stated Ellison.

Suddenly they both looked back over their shoulders westward at two dirt bikes as they roared onto the scene, jumping into the air from a peak a half a football field away. They both smiled.

How fun.

"What day is it, Amos?"

"Friday."

"It's your town. What do you wanna do?"

He shrugged his shoulders and laughed. He was so glad to be out of that place, this was heaven.

"You know what?"

"What?" Amos replied.

"I got an idea."

The sky was dark by now, with just a glint of light above the horizon. The crowds had formed at the grassy park in town, and the speakers next to the stage played pop music as people shopped and ate and milled about, rubbing shoulders with neighbors and friends, tourists and strangers who were in town for the occasion or just passing through.

A band took the stage, and broke into a single they were promoting at other events around the state, and with as much notoriety as the prerecorded songs. Ellison and Amos slipped up the stairs, and behind the curtains that laced the side behind the library. Ellison stopped to listen intently.

The singer had a really good voice, definitely a tenor. He watched as the crowds began walking toward the stage. Kids ran to look at the musicians, as others ran in circles until their moms and dads took their arms. More intently, were the college age students and teenagers who watched the performers with both critical and relaxed eyes, some moving to the beat of the drum, others acting like it were the most mundane thing in life.

Ellison finally turned back to Amos, and smiled.

"I like it. You have your cell phone?"

"Yeah."

"Good. I need you to be my stage manager tonight."

"What!" he said not believing his ears which were competing with the music.

Just as the song finished, and the singer introduced themselves, Ellison walked up to one of the band's entourage off-stage. The man looked confused a moment, then his face went blank. He ran out onto the stage and up to the singer just as they hit the first note of the next song.

The band stopped and the singer looked where the man was pointing, at Ellison.

"Hang on, folks," he said into the microphone, and walked offstage.

"My gosh. Hi, I'm Michael," the singer said to Ellison.

"Does you band know any of our music?"

"Sure, but not practiced."

"Do you know the words to 'The Great Ideal?'"

"Yeah, I think so."

"How would you like every cell phone in the audience who wants, to post us playing that song on You Tube?"

"Uh, yeah. That would be awesome."

"I need that guitar, if that's okay."

Ellison smiled big as he pointed to the guitar offstage. A beat passed as Ellison followed the singer onto the stage. Michael went to the drummer and mouthed words to him. The guitarist looked at Ellison like he'd seen a ghost, and the bass guitar man did a double-take as Ellison retraced his steps where Amos watched, and who's expression was of total marvel.

"Amos. Call 911 and ask them if they can send a couple cops."

Ellison went to the stage again, while tuning the guitar, the sound of his tuning amplified through the park. The other band members followed, as the drummer ran through a series of starts and stops himself, trying to find the rhythm. Suddenly there was a hush, followed by a murmur, and some of the adult males in the back stated moving closer for a look.

"One, two, a one, two, three, four," said the singer.

Ellison's guitar kicked into life, like an awakened beast in sync with the rest of the band. Fortunately, the speakers weren't loud like a concert, but there was a definite change in the tone of the audience. As expected, several males made a mad rush next to the stage with their camera phones high in the air, shouting at one another in wild disbelief.

Amos spoke into his cell phone backstage.

"Hello. Uh, Ellison Watson from Blaze of Glory just joined a local band on stage here at the park. Do you think you could send a couple uniforms to stand guard?"

He listened intently to the voice over the phone.

"No, this isn't a crank call. You want my number?"

A moment passed.

"I guess it was impromptu."

Thirty seconds later, the band got to the guitar solo, as more and more people crowded the stage, heads bobbing, and air guitars followed each note. At the end, the crowd cheered, as Ellison shouted another song at the other players. The singer and guitarist asked him a technical question before they answered. Ellison looked at the drummer, and read his expression.

"Well. You'll have to do the best you can," he mumbled to himself.

"JAFD," he thought.

He went up to him, and mouthed out the main melody in beats, and hoped that did the trick. It did. The start of the next song was hairy, but the drummer picked it up soon after. Ellison played five songs in all with the band and one at the end when he performed a guitar medley. After it finished, he went to the microphone, just as two police officers walked to each side of the stage.

Ellison waited for the shouts and cheers to settle.

"Thank you. Thank you. Thanks to this wonderful band that humored me with this intrusion. I would ask them to finish their set. Umm..."

He looked at Amos, then the crowd.

"This year has been the toughest time in my life, as some of you may know. Uh... I'm not used to speaking."

He looked out at the strangers in the crowd.

"You're not strangers, we're not strangers. We're all family. Like a family that has been away from home. I sense that this is home. Please treasure the strangers among you."

He looked at Amos.

"You might find that the stranger standing next to you, can become your best friend. Thank you."

Ellison exited stage left.

Chapter Thirty-five
Sofie's Choice

The campus was full of life, and Amos was slightly envious as he watched the students go from class to class from the vantage point of the local coffee shop. He wore a new set of clothes, and a pair of Harley Davidson harness style boots he'd always wanted.

The world is my campus now.

He took the check for $120,000 out of the inside pocket of his Harley jacket, which was a deep olive canvas with strips of tan leather. He found both at his favorite Los Angeles location, Universal City Walk. The check had never been folded.

Now I have something to offer her.

He replaced the check and looked at the two tickets to a local Company of Thieves concert, and smiled. Then he took the last sip of his Chai latte and set the ceramic cup on the front counter.

"Thank you," he said to the barista.

Amos had flown to Chicago with the $10,000 reward from the bank. It had financed his new clothes, too. He felt he didn't need a lot. When he got around to cashing the check, he'd probably buy a Prius, or maybe a Subaru. Where he settled depended on Sofie. He could write anywhere. He also looked forward to paying his 10%.

He dialed the number Sofie had given him that was saved on his phone. It went to voicemail. He knew she was a freshman, but she could be anywhere. So he went to the side of campus he figured she might pass by, and sat down near the path at a bench in the middle of buildings, and opened his book. But it wasn't Carl Jung or Jean Jacques Rousseau. It was a fictional story, with no particular theme or message. It was just a good book, with love and conflict, and well-written descriptions of things... Or so he had heard.

From time to time, he'd looked up expecting her face in the crowd. This happened especially between classes. Then he'd focus more on reading. By page 34 or 35, he was hooked. The characters were so rich and real, and he began to forget about why he was there. And then suddenly...

"Amos!"

He looked up to see Sofie standing there next to him, with a huge smile on her face, books in her arms, and wonder in her eyes.

"Hello."

"What are you doing here? Wow. Nice jacket."

Amos stood.

"Thanks," he said as she gave him a once over with her eyes. "How is school?"

"Good. Really good. Have you... Did you come all the way out here for me?"

"Naw. I just wanted to see how all those parents put their hard-earned money to use."

His smile was big and genuine, and then he took a hundred dollar bill out of his pocket, and put it into the front pocket of her pants. Sofie laughed. He turned slightly to the side.

"This is really great."

His free hand waved out at the buildings.

"Well, its home now. I live in the dorms so I don't worry about cooking or anything. My parents came out last weekend to say 'hi.' And I'm just enjoying being a kid for the first time in my life."

"I'm so happy for you, Sofie. You look so beautiful."

He looked from her eyes to her lips, and wanted to kiss her as she smiled back at him, and looked from his eyes, to his lips. Then she stopped smiling, moved to him, and kissed him with her lips closed. They held the kiss for a long moment.

When they parted, he noticed that her eyes were watery, and he looked at her perplexed. He was about to form words when she suddenly spoke first.

"I have to get to class, Amos. I will always love you, okay?"

His expression changed, and she read it like a book.

"Goodbye."

She took his hand in hers and squeezed it, and then a tear ran down her cheek. She suddenly turned and walked off in a rush, her left hand brushing the tear away like swatting a fly. She was gone.

Amos stood motionless for some time, his mouth partly open, his body numb. He didn't see anyone walking past him, as people wondered why he was there by himself, frozen like a statue. The first thing he felt as he came back to life was the sun on the side of his face.

It seemed to thaw him as time passed. The crowds of students became sparser, and it was if he were alone again.

By the time the feeling returned to his legs, he walked back the way he came. As he watched his movements, each turn, each nuance of tree or bush, each person he passed seemed to betray his existence. He got back to the coffee shop and sat down in the sun, which continued it's thawing effect. Would it take a long time to reach his heart?

A couple sat down near him on the patio, and he watched them. He was a writer again, observing life, but not participating. He was invisible. But then his mind took over, and forced his emotions back.

I have friends.

He formed a plan of action, and looked over at the two lovebirds getting up to leave.

"Hey, are you guys busy tonight?"

They turned toward him.

"Why?" asked the guy.

"I have these tickets I don't need."

He reached his hand out, and the girl took them.

"Ah, Company of Thieves! I love them!" she exclaimed.

"Good," replied Amos.

"Thank you," they said in unison.

The girl waved the tickets in the air and smiled again as they walked off.

"Good," Amos said aloud.

He sat back down and dialed a number.

"Hey. How are you?"

"Good," said the voice of Ellison on the other end. "How did it go?"

"It didn't. I need to get the hell out of here, but I don't know where to go."

"Understandable. I'm sort of in limbo myself."

"Really?" said Amos looking out at the branches moving in the breeze.

"Yeah. Let me ask you, do you have any desire to go to Belarus? I mean, the timing is right, before the whole polar north gets dumped with snow."

"I can't think of a place on Earth I'd rather be," replied Amos.

"Well, I was waiting for you to call. Why don't you meet me at JFK."

"Yeah. At least I didn't come this far to go back."

"I'll text you my itinerary."

"Okay."

"Can I put you on speaker phone a moment?"

"Sure," replied Amos.

"Can you hear me?"

"Yeah," replied Amos again.

"By the way, do you know how to spell segue?"

"Of course. But how are you using it?"

"In a lyric."

"Oh. Well, it's s-e-g-u-e, but you can also use a thematic style to describe the segue or transition in the poetry, rather than say it. Dream Theater does it well, but there's a danger of doing it too much."

Suddenly, there was laughter in the background, and Amos heard someone else speak.

"Oh my gosh, he is you!"

"That's frightening," said another voice.

"Who's that?" said Amos smiling.

"Just the band."

Amos laughed.

"Hah. The band?" said Amos in disbelief.

"Yeah."

"Including *the* drummer you don't consider 'just another fucking drummer?'"

"Yes."

"Hello. Pleasure to meet you."

"Likewise," two voices replied.

"Okay. See you in New York."

"Okay. Thanks."

"No. Thank you," said Ellison before hanging up.

Chapter Thirty-six
The Enigma

The crowd anxiously awaited the speaker to enter the stage while the press positioned themselves among supporters and campaign workers. Traditional banners hung around the room, but one in particular caught the attention and comments on camera. The banner was not all that different from what you'd expect from a science-fiction movie. It was a representation of Earth but more detail on the western hemisphere, as the rest of the globe was drawn in lighter colors.

The buzz by television personalities focused on negative fears placed on the drawing by Republicans, and that this candidate was anti-American, and his "agenda" was the dissolution of "our way of life."

Before conclusions could be summed up, the candidate made his entrance onto the stage two minutes early. The networks scrambled to cut to the podium as hosts made apologies off camera.

"Hello. Thank you for coming. I would also like to thank those networks for their participation, but most of all, I want to thank the American people for the courage to tune in, especially at a time where words have lost their meaning."

"My name is Shane Purdue, and I am running for President of the United States. By trade I was in corporate sales and marketing. Before we introduced a new product we consulted lawyers for every aspect of copyright and production. When we introduced new products for the FDA, we consulted the doctors who studied every aspect of its use for consumption. Today, I would ask you to go directly to the source for information about exactly what I stand for, and not my enemies. Because they might be your enemies.

"In war, intelligence is the key to conquering an enemy. We are at war, my fellow Americans. And it is a war for control. You wouldn't ask an enemy what he thinks about his enemy. You wouldn't ask his allies what they think about your own country, because you'll get a warped opinion, unsubstantiated by lies and half-truths. You my fellow friends and neighbors are the intelligence's in this war."

"I want to ask you, what do you want from your government? I was watching a Christian channel before Church one day and the minister was in Sardis at the site of ancient ruins which is in a province of modern Turkey. And he made a point that the shops of local Christians were near the other shops of various religions, including a Jewish synagogue, and near where the Romans played sports, inappropriately robed. He implied that this proximity to such different ideas were the cause of wickedness. If we likened this to America, he may be right if we all lived in the local malls across this country."

"But we do not. And we must learn to coexist."

"We have laws, my fellow Americans, to protect each other, to protect our young, and to protect the freedoms each of us are entitled. The freedom of one can be the slavery of another. If you ride the transit system in Los Angeles, you'd see people trampling on one another's rights daily, because of inappropriate language and aggressive behavior. But what do we do, put policeman on each bus and train?"

"The cure is so simple, though the restructure of our country complex. It is a cure that will heal the dysfunction of America, so psychologically deprived people don't take out their ills upon elementary school children, so triggers aren't reached which push desperate people over the edge, so the lives of the jobless and hope of the educated are reached."

"Do you know why people don't change? Because change is harder than making the decision to go with the status quo. Because it's easier to keep voting for people whose banner we flock to which are familiar. Because if we change, we might have to grow; grow personally, grow as a people, and shake off the chains our ancestors were unable to. Change is hard because we would have to learn from the lessons of history, instead of learning for ourselves because this is our first time around."

"I'm here to tell you, that the rich will take care of themselves, or each other. Republicans will look out for other Republicans. And yes, Democrats will do the same when it comes down to it."

"But we know what that brass ring looks like. We've imagined it, we've flocked to the movies to dream about it. But would we rather live in a dystopia? If we wanted streets made of gold, couldn't we pave it? If we wanted a world imagined in fiction like Star Trek, couldn't we have it?"

"The two parties must unite, and we must do it now. Each must concede, and focus on the positive. The only way we can do this is to bring down the rich to meet the middle man, and raise the poor to the middle class. Isn't it worth it, to choose to be equal. Not by storming the castle, but by allotting to each man, and each family with what he needs by consensus. Or would we rather a different scenario like nuclear war to inspire mankind to change and make the right choice? Or a prolonged depression?"

"I have a plan. We have the technology to do it, to find balance in the temporal and spiritual world we live. Is it not moral to do what is right, and improve our morale as a whole nation? Not usurp authority, but raise the bar. 'One more dead, is one more than it ought to be.'"

"I recommend we change our world by expanding our social service departments on each state level. The problem with government is, it doesn't take the individual into account, because of the limitation of law. The law is here to serve the people, not the other way around. A blanket law in the state of Georgia takes away the driver or commercial license of a father for missing one child support payment, thus penalizing the whole family. This is wrong, thus the law is wrong. The man who doesn't fulfill his responsibilities should have the chance to slip, but not fall. And those who do not choose to be a part of our new system, can simply not participate. But under the law, you cannot just sit at home, watch daytime television, and drink beer, or face the consequences of forfeiting your inheritance, so to speak."

"We need to change our whole infrastructure, so we can preserve our society and prevent loss of life. What is the worth of a soul?"

"What do we have to lose? 'What is man, that thou art mindful of him?' And where has our sense of adventure gone? We don't explore our own solar system. We don't even have the shuttle program. And how many lost their jobs at the closure of ATK? I tell you that modern man is dead or a coward. I say this sarcastically, in the spirit of reverse psychology. We are not dead, but we have let dead hearts, and more so, dead minds lead us nowhere."

"If the God of heaven returned tomorrow, what would be our claim? Are we the good and faithful servant? Or do we live in fear, and practice fear? Are we scared little children who hind our talents?"

"We need a leader who will tell you what you don't want to hear. Isn't that exciting? We need a leader who sees what can be and inspires you to reach for heaven. We need a leader who can walk the line and see both sides, and not meander to and fro, and get nowhere."

"I am that leader. I have to be, to be true to myself. Be true to yourself come Election Day, and we will fulfill the dream of Abraham Lincoln and Thomas Jefferson, and live in a free world that is made up of different people, with different points of view. Not like Sardis, bullied by Rome or another example of tyranny. But men equal in the possibility that the world can dare to be different."

"Then we will see if the rest of the world follows us. Now that is a world worth fighting for. Let us prove them wrong, when they say, America is divided. Thank you."

Chapter Thirty-seven
Encore

Ellison insisted they go 1st class, which was decadent to Amos. He also wanted to pay him back for Alaska. But Ellison refused. So Amos was plotting other ways to do so.

"Did you show her the check?"

"No. If it made a difference, I think it would have... it would have been the wrong motive."

"Good boy."

Amos laughed. He stretched his legs out and marveled at the difference first class was.

"Everyone should go first class, at least once."

"You think your anonymity will be safe as a writer?"

"Probably. I don't need the temptation you must go through."

"What do you mean?"

"Being in the limelight must open too many doors."

"Not if you're grounded."

"That's why I wouldn't marry an actress. I admire their ability, but..."

"But?"

"But it would be tempting for the novelty of a relationship to wear off. I mean, really, how could being married to Scarlett Johanssson get old?"

"I see your point, but the relationship probably wasn't based on what's real to begin with," said Ellison.

"That's why we failed."

"We who?"

"Me and Sofie. It was based on heat. Love at first sight only works when there's more than sex involved."

"Sure that's true, but what's going to prevent that happening with Asya?"

"I'm not going to sleep with her... 'til."

"Hum. Probably a good plan."

Amos looked out the window of the huge jet, and closed his eyes.

"Did the studio give you a time frame to complete The Hate in My Eyes?"

"It's contractually to start production within 5 years."

"What about what you gave me to read?"

"It'll get a new Mac when I get back, and finish."

"Hum."

Amos turned and smiled at Ellison.

"And you?"

Ellison shrugged his shoulders.

"Keep rockin'. What else?"

"Cool. Can't wait..."

Ellison closed his eyes and thought of what was ahead of him. He thought about Katya, and whether their goals were in sync. He felt that ping of pain in his heart at the thought of it not working out.

No matter how old I get...

Love was a risk, and he thought how he and Amos weren't all that different. He would know. After all, he had experience. He would listen to his heart and mind universally. And he would not let Katya forget how important it was having loved so deeply.

At least I have a confirmed date to St. Petersburg.

"Amos?"

He hadn't noticed him dozing off.

"Yes?" he said looking over.

"Why do religious people talk about God like... so much?"

"You know the phrase, misery loves company?"

"Of course."

"Well."

"Well, what?"

"It's the opposite, like finding the cure to cancer. Wouldn't you share it?"

"Gotcha. Or should I say 'word.'"

Ellison laughed. Amos shook his head.

"Please."

"Hey. I'm hip."

"No, you're not. If you were, I wouldn't want anything to do with you."

Ellison smiled and played it over in his head.

If misery loves company... the world would be exactly as it is.

The End

Poetry or prose is a fine art best appreciated in small quantities. Blowing through a book of poetry like you would a novel is counterproductive because then there's little reflection. It is the thoughts that poetry produces that make feelings what they are by words on the page, the imagery or the trains of thoughts poetry produces.

(I publish the following words, and do so for "one" person, knowing full well we cannot communicate **all we are** at once.)

Black & White

One road doesn't seem fair, to expect everyone to toe the line.
What a disappointment I must be, thinking I am your foe.
You think you know everything, just because of one word?
Does that word label me, like the experience of just one day?

I don't know you, but you're a puzzle that intrigues me.
Your past, how you got here, and why you made these choices.
I compare you to the stories that serve as models,
But barely typifying you in any way that's fair to reason.

You are beautiful beyond words, and I long for you.
In every way, you hold me captive, but not as you think.
Yes, sex is a part of it, calling to the love I've lacked in life.
But at some point you'd be done with me, like old underwear.

While I'm new you'd admire how I fit you, and love me.
But your attention is easily drawn to other experience.
I would be compared to, seen for my faults, and thrown away
Because you haven't learned 'love,' and don't know yourself.

If you knew that, you'd find a different psychology in love.
You'd see worth in a way very sensitive in spirit.
Do you know you have one, so unique in every way imaginable?
But you're hopping beds, and will another 15 years before it's old.

So here we are at the beginning, on the subject of the "universal me."
You're gone and you'll never be there again.
After all the time we spent, you still don't know who I am.
But I know you because I was settled to find out more...

Weakness

I stare in the mirror and see who is inside from that first thought
to every wall, emotional tragedy, and triumph that kept me alive.
It certainly isn't fair but that place that unifies us in all nature
also makes me love you, just as I love the forested mountains.

Do you know why half the world is so lonely, without hope?
When you love someone and leave them, who heals them?
When you get used to being there, it shocks the soul.
The other half never learn, until they fall, and miss what could have
been.

I see myself as eternal while you laugh at me across the world.
How do I typify all you see like that one road prescribed?
I am used up 'yes,' thrown aside with the best parts of me.
But my weakness is made strong, and you weren't there to see.

I went along those mountain roads feeling the wind pass easily.
Inside I beat the shit out of what I hated and longed for change.
Towns and cities gave me courage like a whole new story.*
Still lost but knowing exactly what I want, from someone else.

If only we could redefine neuropath ways like scientists view
in a microscope or genetic sequence of dashes on the page.
It would take a god to know each one, and how it came to be**
But that's how love is grown, it disciplines and sharpens.

So what you saw as black and white, a narrow path to control,
is a waste of time on your part, lives shattered and used.
Like a prostitute who should have been adorned with jewels
instead of abused behind glass or plastic, celluloid and DVDs...
      The path wasn't a path at all
      but a wavy line that crisscrosses
      the lines of black and white

[*instead of using people like props and puppets]
[**How did I become self-aware to know this universe
if not more than what is generally thought about us]

Whore & Bastards

For every whore in the world, exits hundreds more bastards
In the age of feminism, why do women not see men?
For what we are, is what we think?
But if you're right, my labels a pack of lies?
Then answer me this, when does innocence die?

Does it die at 8, when dad taught you to shoot?
Or 12, when Kim let you pop her "cherry?"
Was it the little nuances and examples along the way?
while sports taught you not to be a fairy?

I'll tell you exactly when you forgot who you were,
when the childlike innocence left your soul.
It was when you stopped being 'cute' for the price of being handsome
And the million other times you forgot you're anything special.

Who said this was the best we can do?
Who said happiness is a conquest?
You just advertise to all the world that to have any class
means other people have to be put down under shoe.

I can imagine quite easily a revolution worth fighting
When animalistic behaviors are replaced by generous giving.*
And rewards are not stolen by climbing to the top.
Why do you think 'freedom' means you have the right to behave badly?

But who's to decide what's bad, or that's not good?
Do you agree that Socrates, Plato, and Aristotle should?
The reason this country is worse than many others
is the idea that we're better, so arrogant.**

[*yet we're worse than animals because of greed]

191

[**just because of germs, guns, and steel
  not to mention two oceans which separate us]

Evolution

Finding myself full 'circle' to Black & White,
completing it is knowing yourself for the first time.
If thought a foe because of one word,
who's a more finite thinker?

Why is your box so small?
And why do you limit the human mind at all?
You're still the one to say
"You can't believe that way."

[Like the song "Someday, when we are wiser,"
How can we ever be something we aren't?
living the same length of lives as those before us
and making the same selfish mistakes as generations gone by?]

If I'm a child with infantile thoughts,
Why do I hold true to such reason?
As a child born to religion, reawakened by science,
born again to philosophy, I evolved by all 4 seasons.

Deeply overshadowed by the last, final battle.
Inner being frozen by the winter of existential angst.
My baby self is crying from all the pain and suffering.
Fighting each day to be more psychologically.

Ever evolving isn't just the catch phrase of the day
It's a necessity out of total boredom, not elitism.
So don't confuse it for being a know-it-all,
rather be a smart-ass, than a dumb-one. ;)

What a lovely thought that would be
Surrounded by Paradisiacal beauty walking hands clasped
With your loveliness beside me forever

A new Adam on a fresh world; you as my Eve.
This time with full recollection of our past.

Golden Age

It's impossible to escape that trap of life
Set amidst depression and economic drought
Caught in the incessant thoughts flooding in at 3 am
Each day temptation to give up a lost battle fought.

This is the sore disease of the poor
All I want to do is run away from myself
Even in the presence of discovery and silver linings
Being faithful means holding onto the smallest sliver of hope

What is it like to be someone else
With a whole different set of experiences?
Like Blake I've crossed that line from innocence
to a world of experience I wish to shut out.

No matter where I look, I see problems and solutions
The people who make a difference, are so busy not
and unconscious of their traps of never-ending woe,
that new problems form before old ones solved.

Am I the only one to see repetitions in human history?
The frail and innocent as vulnerable as days of revolutions.
Princess and the pea sleeps in every home.
My only comfort are songs of perfect melancholy.

Million dollar condos surrounding Central Park.
Almost 200 grand deep in Latino neighborhoods
The worst it gets, the better for them
To prey on the middle and lower parts.

Remembering

It would take a life as an amoeba
to appreciate life as a worm
It would take the life of a wheel bug
to appreciate life as a frog

It would take the life as a snake
to appreciate life as a mongoose
Or life as a rabbit
to appreciate life as a bold eagle

It would take a life as a monkey
to appreciate life as a human
Or life as a human
to appreciate it as a criminal

It would take a life as a dolphin
to appreciate it over a shark
Or life as a philanthropist
to appreciate life as a dictator

It would take a human to know an unfair comparison
or a weak-minded fool to escape any sense of consciousness
It would take an O.J. Simpson to become a Charles Manson
or a Gandhi to become a Christ

Aristotle or Hitler cannot become a cow or Earthbound fowl
Wisdom is learned but not taught
The choices we make determine the speed of thought
Gathering morale intelligence is primarily how

LUCID

Funny to start an empty page
After reading Whitman & Blake
But the poem running through my mind
Is the creation of my own kind

It's a horror never experienced
A loathing of self never felt
It's an awareness that alienated people
That makes your wings so oblique and steep

Mountains and women are connected so strongly
You think you've seen it all to find a new mold
Both are earth-shattering to an empty heart
It only takes one to build a home most lovely

Purposefully disjointed like the words of a song
Each segue and stanza tuned to a different rung
As lucid and fluid as a raging river
The strings of a guitar that make the heart quiver

Such is the sacrifice knowing God
And reading man's heart deep below the surface
Is an invisible road map with an unknown purpose
Becoming His equal a misunderstood command to be perfect

Sometimes I don't see how choices brought me here
Half the time spent living in fear
The absence of Love my only real weakness
Forty years looking & living inside made a quantifiable difference

Alina

Oh, Alina. How easy I see your face in my mind.
Your smile such a match to my heart
there is no denying your loveliness and beauty
your elegance and grace like no other kind.

I abandon those memories of years gone by
and all the heartbreaks mean nothing.
The promise of you like a rebirth,
Like a child on Christmas morning.

The lights in my eyes in the night's sky
remind me of the sparkle in your smile,
behind your eyes a voice says you're mine,
a fashion design of earth tones so smooth & mild.

Our cultures miles away, mirror the other
Where esoteric and literal form the cosmos
Love is bound in hearts broken in two
But cross planes of space and unite heavens

The snow shines in the bright sun for you
Trees breathe exuberant exhales when you're near
Writers in history fail to capture your character
But I see you like no other in the arms of destiny

I smell the way your hair flows about your shoulders
I hear your laugh in native accents of innocence
You make my heart see worlds yet uncreated & sublime
A single kiss of your lips would stop time & my heart.

Little Jewish Girl

Hello little Jewish girl with smiles for everyone
Your face is much more expressive than most
Your eyes twinkle with acceptance and question
You work to brighten everyone on the payroll today

We fall at your feet under an accent so sweet
Our hearts go a flutter on entering a room
The petite nature a giant become
And glances a beam of light from love

Who will you choose in the pageant of life?
And compliment your exquisite sensibilities
Within your blood generations on trial
And scourged despite infinite possibilities

Do not steal from her what is most precious
And require less from yourself
If you can't love her forever
Your advances are ultimately suspicious

Don't be jealous Syria & Algeria
Would you trade places with the little Jewish girl?
Would you be sacrificed for a heaven?
By those who covet and chastened from above?

It is a daily occurrence to squander the flock
Forget what is inside for a life of hate
But the little Jewish girl has forgotten
Who she was at any rate.

Cry for her soul who is sold for silver
And forget the stars that sing upon her return

Infinity with Carl Jung

Is it wrong for the individual or those representing the individual, to lose certain freedom for the price of social harmony and welfare? By the word certain, to be defined as, individuals focusing on the greater good of the masses, rather than the specific whims of the individual. After all, total freedom to the masses or individuals would result in chaos.

Part 1: Here is the Infinite described using a quote by Carl Jung as the springboard: "Since scientific knowledge not only enjoys universal esteem but, in the eyes of modern man, counts as the only intellectual and spiritual authority, understanding the individual obliges me to commit lese majeste," (crime against supreme rule) "so to speak, to turn a blind eye to scientific knowledge.

Part 2: "This is a sacrifice not lightly made, for the scientific attitude cannot rid itself so easily of its sense of responsibility. And if the psychologist happens to be a doctor who wants not only to classify his patient scientifically but also to understand him as a human being, he is threatened with a conflict of duties between the two diametrically opposed and mutually exclusive attitudes of knowledge, on the one hand, and understanding, on the other."

Part 3: "This conflict cannot be solved by an either-or but only by a kind of two-way thinking: doing one thing while not losing sight of the other."

Part 4: "In view of the fact that in principle, the positive advantages of knowledge work specifically to the disadvantage of understanding, the judgment resulting therefrom is likely to be something of a PARADOX. Judged scientifically, the individual is nothing but a unit which repeats itself ad infinitum and could just as well be designated with a letter of the alphabet."

Part 5: "For understanding, on the other hand, it is just the unique individual human being who, when stripped of all those conformities and regularities so dear to the heart of the scientist, is the supreme and only real object of investigation. The doctor, above all, should be aware of this contradiction."

Part 6: ..."Scientific education is based in the main on statistical truths and abstract knowledge and therefore imparts an unrealistic, rational picture of the world, in which the individual, as merely a marginal phenomenon, plays no role. The individual, however, as an irrational datum, is the true and authentic carrier of reality, the concrete man as opposed to the unreal ideal or normal man to whom the scientific statements refer." The Undiscovered Self

Part 7: Thesis: If therefore it is possible for man to comprehend opposites, which are both true, specifically mentioned science & psychology, then seeing both pov's as concepts, adding to the contemplative nature of man's ability, then it proves that there is a nature of man that is infinite, though this may not apply to all mankind as comprehensively as others who have evolved thus.
Were he capable to continue on, his experience would be essential in comprehending infinity.

"And experience the flight
Just try to see from a different side
If balance is the key
Then maybe we'll see a future understanding."
         Queensryche, My Global Mind

When we look at a child, he or she demands specific attention.
And we look at them so admirably, it is no real sacrifice.
And yet if we look at the child all grown up,
Then somehow that individual loses value to us.
This is a huge misconception, for the child continues inside
Even though the image of innocence may be lost.

Conclusion: As difficult it is for the human mind to see two different points of view simultaneously, how much more infinite is the brain that's "wired" to see five, or even seven?

What others see from their pov as an objection, another sees as a connection to every facet in life. Why is their box so small? Choice, or better yet, freewill. It depends on your pov whether you see truth being scattered, or truth being everywhere. Can you believe that it's enough? You don't need more?

Fear

Fear. Fear is the most debilitating emotion. Fear of loss of money by govt. Fear of freedom lost. Fear of a belief system we don't share. Fear of psychology because we do not want to change. Fear of science because it might disprove our beliefs. Fear that someone might possess something we do not; faith, happiness, materials possessions, power, etc. Fear that our prejudices are debunked. Fear our football team doesn't win. Fear that our weakness may be exposed... Fear is a lie. Fear leads to dissension and contention. Fear breeds hate. Hate leads to loss of hope. Loss of hope alienated us from one another causing loneliness. Fear divides like no other emotion.

Fear prevents us from feeling something previously beyond our experience. Fear prevents a spiritual experience. Fear prevents greater awareness and growth. Fear promotes finiteness or linear thinking. Fear prevents us from seeing other points of view. Fear prevents us from seeing every facet of life, and prevents growth in these areas. Prefect Love casts out fear. Fear prevents balance. Fear creates left wings and right wings. Fear prevents us from seeing the Whole Enchilada.

Origin of Man

"Luke. You're going to learn that many of the truths we cling to depend greatly on our own point of view." Fact: There were at least 3 origins of man, maybe more. One: Out of Africa. Two: Out of Mesopotamia, between the Tigris and Euphrates Rivers (modern-day Iraq, ironically), and from God (Adam & Eve).

If God were not the author of all 3, they could not have thrived in existence. Especially those from Africa. Can you imagine how the beasts of the jungle would have exacted its natural inclination to feed on defenseless humans prior to the invention of warfare, namely the lance, a sharpened staff, or other (also demonstrated in the film 2001: A Space Odyssey). Neanderthal man could not have lasted against any of the beasts at the time, despite the fact dinosaurs were long gone.

DaVinci Code

If Jesus wasn't divine, why would it matter if Mary Magdelane was with child, or of the royal bloodline, as The DaVinci Code portrays? And what difference would it make for the Church?

The fact that Catholicism reigned in terror against women, established the monastic order and celibacy, and showed no similarity to the Primitive Church with apostles proves it is a church of man, Constantine.

"Each breathe you take is a sin, woman." Again the fallacy of men which teach the creation of God could be anything but divine, or he is flawed himself. "... to bring to pass the eternal life of man."

What does pagan ritual have to do with transcendence, other than Constantine's participation in the Nicene Creed & trinity's 3 in 1?

Human is divine...

Isaiah 53: 5 "But he was wounded for our transgressions, he was bruised for our iniquities: the chastisement of our peace was upon him; and with his stripes we are healed."
-700 B. C.

Modern Politics

Just over a year ago I was selling replacement windows door to door in Utah, seeing homes foreclosed, talking to people losing their homes because of the job market. I just saw Mitt Romney say "to let the foreclosure market run its course so it can rebound." This is his solution? Doesn't he know that those are families losing their homes? I wouldn't vote for this ass if he were the only one running. He's not a "Mormon." Not according to the scriptures I can quote. I am totally disgusted.

I guess the lesson in life I just can't learn is letting the harsh realities be heaped upon good people without wanting to do something to make things better. Definitely not a Republican. There lies the will of God, to feed the poor, visit the widow, cloth & house the homeless, be undefiled by money and the world, i.e. "pure religion. Proverbs 19:17 "He that hath pity upon the poor lendeth unto the Lord; and that which he hath given will he pay him again."

"You are either to abolish slavery or it will abolish you." - Whitman on the south. America will either abolish inequality, or inequality will abolish you. No more kings, of fortune. - Gibbons on the class system.

Why do we prescribe our hypocrisies upon the Founding Fathers as if they would agree to them. I dare say they would be more critical, because their goal was to limit power and allow a level playing field, at least in many areas. Neither is being practiced, because inequality reigns. The Great Experiment of America has run its course. We have now the responsibility to
establish Utopia, which has never had a chance before. Technology makes it real for the first time because of our ability to produce food for the world and the means of distributing it. That's just one example. Forget "communism."

Utopia as prescribed by Thomas More, Plato, and yes, even Gene Roddenberry.

I pledge allegiance to the truth and universality of the Earth. And to the Republics for which divide; one equality, one humanity, one planet under God, indivisible, with liberty and justice for all. - United Federation of Earth.

Two inequalities: One by nature, and another, by the consent of men. This latter consists of the different privileges which some men enjoy to the prejudice of others; such as that of being more rich, more honored, more powerful, or even in a position to exact obedience... "Are those who command necessarily better than those who obey?" - Rousseau

If I stand for nothing else, it is the thought which attribute that human beings can be simple minded, but understanding the paradox, what Carl Jung described as two opposites which both are true, can catapult the human consciousness to divine levels...

We fear what we don't understand. We don't understand what is different. What is different is what is not experienced. What is not experienced is being finite. What is finite is not seeing other pov's. Not seeing other pov's is what being human is all about. Being human is about fearing the unknown. Fearing the unknown is the opposite of the concept and belief of God. Fearing the unknown is the opposite of Love. Loving others is the application of Spiritual Principles.

Maybe the way I see the world isn't the way you do. But if my vision becomes reality, everyone would be happier than they are now. So how could that be a bad thing? I know. You'd still piss and moan if that's your nature.

"Poverty is the parent of revolution and crime." -Aristotle

Prejudice is taught in every level but to an evolved, open mind. A child is taught one to protect them or because of a parent's weakness and adults adopt them to make sense of the world. But truth is understanding why the differences are vehicles of learning...

Every day we do nothing to overhaul the government in this country to one that disperses needs equally based on family size and create utopia as described by Thomas More and Jean Jacques Rousseau, the more good people and children will suffer; not just for want of food but depression. I am one of them.

There is a cycle of behavior the insensitive repeat over and over again who claim they are not "hurting" anyone. And they sometimes criticize those who "know" it is immoral. These are they who act as fillers in society and experience differences those who believe in a higher power do not. Thus they progress much slower. Higher intelligence does not denote money, power, education, or fame.

Which is why the "childlike" are not afraid to learn the lessons those who fear real change do.

There may not be nothing new under the sun, but putting the pieces together again may remind us of what didn't stick the last time around.

"I just feel all I do all day long is manage myself. Try to connect with people. But no matter how much energy you pour into it, there's no guarantee anyone's going to be there for you." Six Feet Under - Nate. Thus is the desperate state of those without hope.

Beauty is in the heart. Life is the journey to make the world into what the heart knows it should be. Wanting or expecting something for nothing is an entitlement attitude that fosters elitism. Ironically, it applies to both rich and poor. One is greed. The other is the epidemic and nature of the desperate.

Sometimes the lessons of life are not to act perfectly, but to act perfectly when genuinely wronged, unjustifiably.

Somewhere between Abraham Lincoln and Dwight Eisenhower, the Republican party changed dramatically, just as Communism elicited fear upon the world as a tyrannical byproduct of W.W.II. Fear has become the name of the game since.

Even elections of Nixon and W. could not demonstrate the contradiction of the symbiosis of the Super-rich and religion. If we cannot differentiate ourselves from the doctrines of the world, and the complex subtlety of this hypocrisy, then the division between the Democratic Party and its half-truths will be upon our own conscience. This division is accelerated by renewed fervor and fanatics like the Tea Party. The sign of our gullibility is having men like Mitt Romney who reverberate the same party finiteness.

Example: It is prejudice to pick on the flaws of the poor as if it exceeds the ambition of the hardworking rich as they prey on society in the name of capitalism. Government's checks and balances were designed to curtail usurpation of power, which is exactly what money buys.

The poverty stricken mind is depressed, while the feeding frenzy of the rich are like piranha devouring everything it can get its mouths on. To criticize someone for taking advantage of welfare, or any other programs, means that they do not see all of human nature, and fail to do so in opposite perspectives. There needs to be both

208

checks and balances as well as incentives to "inspire" production, not just as the free meal on your break at Burger King.

Saving face often prevents people from doing the right thing. The bigger the ego, the harder the repentance. Being right is a defense mechanism that prevents emotional and spiritual growth.

Observation: During 2004 Election, I went into each party Office in Simi Valley stating I was the opposite affiliation. The Dems were the more receptive. That hostility demonstrated by Reps are as evident with Dems on a day to day basis on religion.

Proof that preconceived notions are applied rather than on a case by case basis. I quoted Henry David Thoreau once to a man I played chess with on weekends in LA, and he immediately invoked all the hostility he felt for religion because of his college instruction, and opinions formulated then. This is hypocrisy, and the fallacy of the party system/finiteness of the human condition.

The "world "sees fractures in crust
And fails to see the strings in each of us
Chasm shifting out of time
In the mind that is not in rhyme

The trees see our mortal plight
But we still fail to see the light
Breathing wisdom extending life
With the freedom to abort.

Finite sees half is right
And doesn't mind cruel nature
Let me disagree with you
I'm just another caricature

I approached a very nice African American man walking slower along the street, when he engaged me in conversation about the snowflakes in the air, and location of homeless shelter if unable to hitch-hike to San Diego. He arrived an hour before from Philadelphia via truck-driver. Answering his questions, he asked me if I could buy him breakfast. After saying I had $5 left to get though the day, we parted ways, and I entered Starbucks setting my computer at a table. On the floor next to the chair was $2, and I ran it out to him along sidewalk. Was it a miracle, or just a coincidence? Or are coincidences miracles?

Truth is sweet like honey. It's everywhere. How can you believe nothing when wherever you look you can see eternity? I know that it's easier for people to talk about the weather, talk about movies, to be like Switzerland. But do we really respect Switzerland? Or do we respect George Washington, Martin Luther King, and Abraham Lincoln? I'd rather be Lincoln, surrounded by stupidity, ignorance, and bigotry than be any one of those things. But at the end of the day, I love you. I care about you. And even if you hate me, I will go on standing for what is right.

DEMOCRATS, Do not be hypocrites like the Republics and say:

Job 21:13 They spend their days in wealth, and in a moment go down to the grave.

14 Therefore they say unto God, Depart from us; for we desire not the knowledge of thy ways.

15 What is the Almighty, that we should serve him? and what profit should we have, if we pray unto him?

Job 20: 10 His children shall seek to please the poor, and his hands shall restore their goods.

11 His bones are full of the sin of his youth, which shall lie down with him in the dust.

12 Though wickedness be sweet in his mouth, though he hide it under his tongue;

Here's the secret no one has told you. Chaos and order exist side by side. We each suffer while in this life, some cause it on themselves and some because they're chastened. But if you Don't Suffer, then you have your reward. For God chastens those he Loves most. Christ suffered so we wouldn't have to, at that magnitude. But we still pay the price so we can learn, and take that knowledge with us.

98.3%. That's the number people really don't believe exactly the way you do on most things. 50%. That's the figure that people who you do agree with really believe something else. 1.7%. That's the number of those who really do get IT. 98%....

We are all beggars. Our "works" may get us to a higher Kingdom, but salvation is a gift, and no matter how much money we

210

make or what we do can change that. When will we as finite beings learn that we each have different talents and experiences?

If Democrats are the swine before pearls, then Republicans are the camel in the eye of the needle.

Psychology

Simply put, psychology is the study of the human mind. A very successful salesman at work told me he did not believe in it. After a few minutes of conversation with me, he admitted to me that I was correctly accessing his behavior toward a given reaction he'd made. Is that progress, or would he ever admit to himself that I applied what he doesn't believe. This is a perfect example of faith, too.

We may or not admit what others accept, or experience, but that is because we have different talents. One reality is mastering certain facets of life. Spirituality is one. Being well rounded is accepting all, at once. To understand the Psychology of God takes a huge brain, conscious effect, and a lot of study, and perception. To see what others do not, especially other Christians, to see things as God sees it, to not judge based on a finite/one-life pov, is essential.

You could no more be an actor playing roles both unnatural and immoral, than a defense attorney defending real criminals. Perhaps for those who do it fulfills its purpose, like the "theory" of reincarnation. Does living such lives afford the lessons to progress, or simply bask in an unrelenting chain of events...

How do you reconcile when two POVs are so diametrically opposed on so many issues? Both feel that compromise on any of their core beliefs is surrender to the opposition. Take Israel and Iran. Iranian leaders would like to destroy Israel and wipe it off the map, killing every single Jew everywhere. How does Israel negotiate against that type of adversary? It's not a matter of sitting around the campfire and singing Kum-bi-ya. One must stand up for their beliefs and that is exactly what is happening. Each side, Liberal Democrat and Conservative feel passionately about the issues at hand.

Answer: That is the error. To think that we are so different, the other pov is so wrong, is so narrow a view. Not you personally. We are so brainwashed to think an enemy is at our gates, that it is personified by our preference in football teams. Or the Olympics are a perfect example. I don't root for Americans alone. We are a universal people. It's arrogant to think otherwise.

This is the message of change that needs to happen...

Ether 8:18 And it came to pass that they formed a secret combination, even as they of old; which combination is most abominable and wicked above all, in the sight of God;

3 Nephi 7:6 And the regulations of the government were destroyed, because of the secret combination of the friends and kindreds of those who murdered the prophets."

Pt. 1- When religion, any religion, or political party, seeks to exercise control to "force" people to do what is right, it is putting the Constitution on the shelf, and practicing authoritarian rule. In religious terms, it is supporting the doctrine of Satan because he wanted to force people to do obey and the credit was his.

Pt. 2- The Constitution was designed to put checks and balances in force to ensure free enterprise, but regulate commerce to ensure equality and the pursuit of happiness. When people imply that it ensures greed and turns a blind eye to financial dynasties, "allowing that 'come what may attitude' to run its course," then this is what God meant by the Constitution hanging by a thread. When Orrin Hatch and Glenn Beck imply they are justified to strip freedom of choice from those who oppose "ultimate" freedoms of corporations, they are playing into the subtleties of Lucifer and stripping the Constitution of its intended power. Just as any Democrat who thinks that ultimate freedom to do wickedness is right. But a spade's a spade.

Conclusion: Stripping freewill in the name of morality, or any other "ism," is contrary to the prime directive of God, so to speak. And it pushes sinners and the poor away from the true gospel. God's opinion is there is little chance for repentance or change with the rich man, or woman.

You think you're smarter than me because I believe in the eternal soul, and the so-called traditions of the past? No. If that were true, I'd neither forge my own way to these conclusions nor not see how everything is connected. I've faced the India where the individual ceases to exist. I've seen the unreality that nothing is real as a Buddhist. I've taken the best of the philosophers like Plato & Aristotle and am not afraid to be uncool in a world that sees flesh, and fame, and indulgence. No one can offer me anything that I don't already have; faith.

You've heard "the heart wants what the heart wants?" Well, the mind craves what the mind craves. For some it's money & power, or sleek physique & sex. For others it's "ever learning but never coming to the knowledge of the truth" or intellectual cynicism for no reason other than to differentiate oneself from the 'norm.' But true knowledge comes from finding balance between the heart & the mind. That centeredness is the only real key to any enlightenment and emotional/intellectual growth.

Why do dramatic stories involving Mormons among the gentile world involve homosexuality, pornography, drug abuse, etc. in every incarnation on film or theater? Angels In America, Orgasmo, even the recent Broadway play Book of Mormon musical. Are these people that desperate to trivialize everything sacred and sublime? Please just use your own pathetic lives as backdrops to entertain yourselves.

On the Outside

Much can be explained in order to understand the author's reason for some aspects of Ellison & Amos, as long as it keeps within the same theme. I don't like it when authors explain away every nuance and detail behind the creation of a work, like Johnny Cheever. In his case, it made it more unbelievable, especially where homosexual behavior is prescribed on a heterosexual male.

Yes, sex can be a delicate topic and very confusing if traumatically experienced. Mine was. But I personally set the highest goals growing up, but got to a point when nothing I had planned in a very stereotypical world went down that way. I would have been totally happy if my life had not defined itself outside the norm. There was even a time when I was perceived as evil by my own, when chemically and physiologically, I was in the middle of a psychological tailspin.

But I would not want my own beloved son, who this book is dedicated, to go at life so alone, and without the love and support I did not have. Both males and females are defined by the roles with their fathers, if you believe the studies out there, and Michael Gurian who authored The Wonder of Boys, and The Wonder of Girls. I do, because I had very little exposure to male role models other than my own community. And regardless to the theories which say it takes a village to raise a child, that's a load of crap if the child doesn't have the family structure in the home.

I never met my father, at birth or otherwise. Then he died when I was five living in Southern California. He had remained in the Chicago area when my mother had left. I naturally developed a strong connection to my Grandpa, and when we visited Boulder City, NV, I was joined at his hip. My fondest memories of childhood was getting up before the sun and joining him for coffee (with lots of cream and sugar, of course).

I remember his funeral like it was yesterday when I was 10. He died of colon cancer. And even though I did have a spiritual bond with the husband of one of my aunts, there were so many negative examples that equally plagued my life beyond the formative years that I did just as Gurian predicted, and withdrew into religion and music, and the power of imagination. The fact that mine was a bully school growing up, I developed quite a temper.

So herein laid the problem at hand. From the earliest memories, I was in love with someone. From Laura Pendergrass in the 1st grade to every name my brain cataloged along the way, that sweet little boy I once was, who I often see in my son now, was so enveloped in that romantic aspect, that it followed me every day.

After my mission, the sacrifice and joy of a year and a half service to God, often times a ball of emotional acrobatics, I found "the one" while working at a shoe store Christmas season before returning to college. She was a senior in high school, and for the first time in my life, we went on perfect date after absolute perfect courtship. I attended a musical she performed at, and felt something that I have never felt since, sealing my fate. But I was still that little boy who was alone, and I missed a step, and without expressing what I did not know myself, lost her.

I had no car, no family, and no experience. Strike three. And even though I had many other chances to marry a girl who I would have been totally happy with, I wasn't sure of them like I was her. So when sex came knocking a few years later, I forgot my goals, who I was, and gave into the overwhelming hormonal need. Thus the fall occurred. As time went on, I can see in hindsight that my choices were for women I psychologically could not have a real relationship with. It was sporadic at best and spanned years in between.

During all this time, I came around to who I was again, but as age sets in, people see you first for who you are on the outside, and rarely do you get a chance to start over like when you were 30, especially if you never find the validation required professionally to support a potential wife.

When we reach for something in our self
We find what's missing in someone else
We're all puzzles missing important parts
That fit the pieces in others' hearts.

The real world isn't what you see outside, but within, because the outside world belongs to people who don't know who you are. Or themselves...

Spirit cannot be created from nothing. Nothing is created from nothing. If it has a beginning, it will have an end... That is why we are kindred to God. And this is life eternal...

We're all the same. Learning how to be who we're going to be.

Charlie Gibbons